A Floating City and the Blockade Runners

Verne, Jules

BIBLIOLIFE

ONE WOULD HAVE TAKEN HER FOR A SMALL ISLAND.

UNIFORM EDITION

A FLOATING CITY

AND

THE BLOCKADE RUNNERS

BY

JULES VERNE

ILLUSTRATED

NEW YORK
CHARLES SCRIBNER'S SONS

LIST OF ILLUSTRATIONS.

A FLOATING CITY.

CHAPTER I.

On the 18th of March, 1867, I arrived at Liverpool, in-
tending to take a berth simply as an amateur traveller on
board the "Great Eastern," which in a few days was to
sail for New York. I had sometimes thought of paying a
visit to North America, and was now tempted to cross the
Atlantic on board this gigantic boat. First of all the
"Great Eastern," then the country celebrated by Cooper.

This steam-ship is indeed a masterpiece of naval construction; more than a vessel, it is a floating city, part of
the country, detached from English soil, which after having
crossed the sea, unites itself to the American Continent. I
pictured to myself this enormous bulk borne on the waves,
her defiant struggle with the wind, her boldness before the
powerless sea, her indifference to the billows, her stability in
the midst of that element which tosses "Warriors" and

B

"Solferinos" like ship's boats. But my imagination carried me no farther; all these things I did indeed see during the passage, and many others which do not exclusively belong to the maritime domain. If the "Great Eastern" is not merely a nautical engine, but rather a microcosm, and carries a small world with it, an observer will not be astonished to meet here, as on a larger theatre, all the instincts, follies, and passions of human nature.

On leaving the station, I went to the Adelphi Hotel. The "Great Eastern" was announced to sail on the 20th of March, and as I wished to witness the last preparations, I asked permission of Captain Anderson, the commander, to take my place on board immediately, which permission he very obligingly granted.

The next day I went down towards the basins which form a double line of docks on the banks of the Mersey. The gate-keepers allowed me to go on to Prince's Landing-Stage, a kind of movable raft which rises and falls with the tide, and is a landing place for the numerous boats which run between Liverpool, and the opposite town of Birkenhead on the left bank of the Mersey.

The Mersey, like the Thames, is only an insignificant stream, unworthy the name of river, although it falls into the sea.

It is an immense depression of the land filled with water, in fact nothing more than a hole, the depth of which allows it to receive ships of the heaviest tonnage, such as the "Great Eastern," to which almost every other port in the world is closed. Thanks to this natural condition, the streams of the Thames and the Mersey have seen two immense commercial cities, London and Liverpool, built almost at their mouths, and from a similar cause has Glasgow arisen on the Clyde.

At Prince's Landing-Stage, a small tug in the service of the "Great Eastern" was getting up steam. I went on board and found it already crowded with workmen and mechanics. As the clock in Victoria Tower struck seven, the tender left her moorings and quickly ascended the Mersey with the rising tide.

Scarcely had we started, when I saw on the quay a tall young man, with that aristocratic look which so distinguishes the English officer. I thought I recognized in him a friend whom I had not seen for several years, a captain in the Indian army; but I must have been mistaken, for Captain Mac Elwin could not have left Bombay, as I ought to have known, besides Mac Elwin was a gay, careless fellow, and a jovial companion, but this person, if he resembled him in feature, seemed melancholy, and as though burdened with a secret grief. Be it as it may, I had not time to observe him more closely, for the tender was moving rapidly away, and the impression founded on this resemblance soon vanished from my mind.

The "Great Eastern" was anchored about three miles up the river, at a depth equal to the height of the tallest houses in Liverpool. She was not to be seen from Prince's Stage, but I caught a glimpse of her imposing bulk from the first bend in the river.

One would have taken her for a small island, hardly discernible in the mist. She appeared with her bows towards us, having swung round with the tide ; but soon the tender altered her course, and the whole length of the steam-ship was presented to our view ; she seemed what in fact she was—enormous! Three or four colliers alongside were pouring their cargoes of coal into her port-holes. Beside the "Great Eastern," these three-mast ships looked like barges ; their chimneys did not even reach the first line of light-ports in her hull ; the yards of their gallant-sails did not come up to her bulwarks. The giant could have hoisted these ships on its davits like shore-boats.

Meanwhile the tender approached the "Great Eastern," whose chains were violently strained by the pressure of the tide, and ranged up to the foot of an immense winding staircase, on the larboard side. In this position the deck of the tender was only on a level with the load water-line of the steam-ship, to which line she would be depressed when in full cargo, and which still emerged two yards.

The workmen were now hurriedly disembarking and clambering up the numerous steps which terminated at the fore-part of the ship. I, with head upturned, and my body thrown back, surveyed the wheels of the "Great Eastern," like a tourist looking up at a high edifice.

Seen from the side, these wheels looked narrow and contracted, although their paddles were four yards broad, but in front they had a monumental aspect. Their elegant fittings, the arrangements of the whole plan, the stays crossing each other to support the division of the triple centre rim, the radius of red spokes, the machinery half lost in the shadow of the wide paddle-boards, all this impressed the mind, and awakened an idea of some gigantic and mysterious power.

With what force must these wooden paddles strike the waves which are now gently breaking over them! what a boiling of water when this powerful engine strikes it blow after blow! what a thundering noise engulfed in this paddle-box cavern! when the "Great Eastern" goes at full speed, under the pressure of wheels measuring fifty-three feet in diameter and 166 in circumference, weighing ninety tons, and making eleven revolutions a minute. The tender had disembarked her crew; I stepped on to the fluted iron steps, and in a few minutes had crossed the fore-part of the "Great Eastern."

CHAPTER II.

THE deck was still nothing but an immense timber-yard given up to an army of workmen. I could not believe I was on board a ship. Several thousand men—workmen, crew, engineers, officers, mechanics, lookers-on—mingled and jostled together without the least concern, some on deck, others in the engine-room; here pacing the upper decks, there scattered in the rigging, all in an indescribable pell-mell. Here fly-wheel cranes were raising enormous pieces of cast-iron, there heavy joists were hoisted by steam-windlasses; above the engine-rooms an iron cylinder, a metal shaft in fact, was balanced. At the bows, the yards creaked as the sails were hoisted; at the stern rose a scaffolding which, doubtless, concealed some building in construction. Building, fixing, carpentering, rigging, and painting, were going on in the midst of the greatest disorder.

My luggage was already on board. I asked to see

CARPENTERING, RIGGING, AND PAINTING.

Captain Anderson, and was told that he had not yet arrived ; but one of the stewards undertook to install me, and had my packages carried to one of the aft. cabins.

" My good fellow," said I to him, " the 'Great Eastern' was announced to sail on the 20th of March, but is it possible that we can be ready in twenty-four hours ? Can you tell me when we may expect to leave Liverpool ? "

But in this respect the steward knew no more than I did, and he left me to myself. I then made up my mind to visit all the ins and outs of this immense ant-hill, and began my walk like a tourist in a foreign town. A black mire— that British mud which is so rarely absent from the pavement of English towns—covered the deck of the steamship; dirty gutters wound here and there. One might have thought oneself in the worst part of Upper Thames Street, near London Bridge. I walked on, following the upper decks towards the stern. Stretching on either side were two wide streets, or rather boulevards, filled with a compact crowd ; thus walking, I came to the centre of the steam-ship between the paddles, united by a double set of bridges.

Here opened the pit containing the machinery of the paddle-wheels, and I had an opportunity of looking at this admirable locomotive engine. About fifty workmen were scattered on the metallic skylights, some clinging to

the long suction-pumps fixing the eccentric wheels, others
hanging on the cranks riveting iron wedges with enormous wrenches.   After having cast a rapid glance over
these fitting works, I continued my walk till I reached
the bows, where the carpenters were finishing the decora-
tion of a large saloon called the " smoking-room," a
magnificent apartment with fourteen windows ; the ceiling
white and gold, and wainscoted with lemon-coloured
panels.   Then, after having crossed a small triangular
space at the bows, I reached the stem, which descends
perpendicularly into the water.

Turning round from this extreme point, through an
opening in the mists, I saw the stern of the " Great
Eastern" at a distance of more than two hundred
yards.

I returned by the boulevards on the starboard side,
avoiding contact with the swaying pulleys and the ropes
of the rigging, lashed in all directions by the wind; now
keeping out of the way, here of the blows of a fly-wheel
crane, and further on, of the flaming scoria which were
showering from a forge like a display of fireworks.   I
could hardly see the tops of the masts, two hundred feet
in height, which lost themselves in the mist, increased by
the black smoke from the tenders and colliers.

After having passed the great hatchway of the engine-
rooms, I observed a " small hotel " on my left, and then

the spacious side walls of a palace surmounted by a terrace, the railings of which were being varnished. At last I reached the stern of the steam-ship, and the place I had already noticed where the scaffolding was erected. Here between the last small deck cabin and the enormous gratings of the hatchways, above which rose the four wheels of the rudder, some engineers had just finished placing a steam-engine. The engine was composed of two horizontal cylinders, and presented a system of pinions, levers, and blocks which seemed to me very complicated. I did not understand at first for what it was intended, but it appeared that here, as everywhere else, the preparations were far from complete.

And now, why all these delays? Why so many new arrangements on board the "Great Eastern," a compara· tively new ship? The reason may be explained in a few words.

After twenty passages from England to America, one of which was marked by very serious disasters, the use of the "Great Eastern" was temporarily abandoned, and this immense ship, arranged to accommodate passengers, seemed no longer good for anything. When the first attempt to lay the Atlantic cable had failed,— partly because the number of ships which carried it was insufficient—engineers thought of the "Great Eastern." She alone could store on board the 2100 miles of metallic wire,

weighing 4500 tons. She alone, thanks to her perfect indifference to the sea, could unroll and immerse this immense
cable. But special arrangements were necessary for storing
away the cable in the ship's hold. Two out of six boilers
were removed, and one chimney out of three belonging to
the screw engine ; in their places large tanks were placed
for the cable, which was immersed in water to preserve
it from the effects of variation of the atmosphere; the
wire thus passed from these tanks of water into the sea
without suffering the least contact with the air.

The laying of the cable having been successfully accomplished, and the object in view attained, the "Great
Eastern" was once more left in her costly idleness. A
French company, called the "Great Eastern Company,
Limited," was floated with a capital of 2,000,000 francs,
with the intention of employing the immense ship for the
conveyance of passengers across the Atlantic. Thus the
reason for rearranging the ship to this purpose, and the con-
sequent necessity of filling up the tanks and replacing the
boilers, of enlarging the saloons in which so many people
were to live during the voyage, and of building extra dining
saloons, finally the arrangement of a thousand berths in
the sides of the gigantic hull.

The "Great Eastern" was freighted to the amount of
25,000 francs a month. Two contracts were arranged
with G. Forrester and Co., of 'Liverpool, the first to the

amount of 538,750 francs, for making new boilers for the screw; the second to the amount of 662,500 francs for general repairs, and fixings on board.

Before entering upon the last undertaking, the Board of Trade required that the ship's hull should undergo a strict examination. This costly operation accomplished, a long crack in her exterior plates was carefully repaired at a great expense, and the next proceeding was to fix the new boilers; the driving main-shaft of the wheels, which had been damaged during the last voyage, had to be replaced by a shaft, provided with two eccentric wheels, which insured the solidity of this important part. And now for the first time the " Great Eastern " was to be steered by steam.

It was for this delicate operation that the engineers intended the engine which they had placed at the stern. The steersman standing on the bridge between the signal apparatus of the wheels and the screw, has before his eyes a dial provided with a moving needle, which tells him every moment the position of his rudder. In order to modify it, he has only to press his hand lightly on a small wheel, measuring hardly a foot in diameter, and placed within his reach. Immediately the valves open, the steam from the boilers rushes along the conducting tubes into the two cylinders of the small engine, the pistons move rapidly, and the rudder instantly obeys. If this plan succeeds a man will be able to direct the gigantic body of the " Great Eastern " with one finger.

For five days operations continued with distracting activity. These delays considerably affected the enterprize of the freighters, but the contractors could do no more. The day for setting sail was irrevocably settled for the 26th of March. The 25th still saw the deck strewn with all kinds of tools.

During this last day, however, little by little the gang- ways were cleared, the scaffoldings were taken down, the fly-wheel cranes disappeared, the fixing of the engines was accomplished, the last screws and nails were driven in, the reservoirs filled with oil, and the last slab rested on its metal mortise. This day the chief engineer tried the boilers. The engine-rooms were full of steam ; leaning over the hatchway, enveloped in a hot mist, I could see nothing, but I heard the long pistons groaning, and the huge cylinders noisily swaying to and fro on their solid swing blocks. The muddy waters of the Mersey were lashed into foam by the slowly revolving paddle-wheels ; at the stern, the screw beat the waves with its four blades ; the two engines, entirely independent of each other, were in complete working order.

Towards five o'clock a small steamer, intended as a shore-boat for the " Great Eastern," came alongside. Her movable engine was first hoisted on board by means of windlasses, but as for the steamer herself, she could not be embarked. Her steel hull was so heavy that the davits to which it was attached bent under the weight, undoubtedly this would not have occurred had they supported them with lifts. Therefore they were obliged to abandon the steamer, but there still remained on the "Great Eastern" a string of sixteen boats hanging to the davits.

Everything was finished by evening; not a trace of mud was visible on the well-swept boulevards, for an army of sweepers had been at work. There was a full cargo; provisions, goods, and coal filled the stewards' room, the store, and the coal houses. However, the steamer had not yet sunk to the load water-line, and did not draw the necessary thirty-three feet. It was an inconvenient position for the wheels, for the paddles not being sufficiently immersed, caused a great diminution in the speed.

Nevertheless it was possible to set sail, and I went to bed with the hope of starting next day. I was not disappointed, for at break of dawn I saw the English, French, and American flags floating from the masts.

CHAPTER III.

THE "Great Eastern" was indeed preparing to sail. Already volumes of black smoke were issuing from the five chimneys, and hot steam filled the engine-rooms. Some sailors were brightening up the four great fog-cannons which were to salute Liverpool as we sailed by. The top-men climbed the yards, disentangled the rigging, and tightened the shrouds on the thick ropes fastened to the barricades. About eleven o'clock the carpenters and painters put the finishing touches to their work, and then embarked on board the tender which awaited them. As soon as there was a sufficient pressure, the steam rushed into the cylinders of the rudder engine, and the engineers had the pleasure of seeing that this ingenious contrivance was an entire success.

The weather was fine, with bright gleams of sunshine darting through the rapidly-moving clouds. There must have been a strong breeze at sea, but we did not feel it.

The officers were all dispersed about the deck, making preparations for getting under sail. The ship's officers were composed of the Captain, the first officer, two assistant officers, five lieutenants, of whom one was a Frenchman, M. H——, and a volunteer who was also French.

Captain Anderson holds a high place in the commercial marine of England. It is to him we are indebted for the laying of the Transatlantic cable, though it is true that if he succeeded where his predecessors had failed, it was because he worked under more favourable circumstances, having the "Great Eastern" at his command. Be it as it may, his success gained for him the title of "Sir." I found him to be a very agreeable commander. He was a man of about fifty years of age, with that tawny complexion which remains unchanged by weather or age ; a thorough Englishman, with a tall figure, a broad smiling face, and merry eyes ; walking with a quiet dignified step, his hands never in his pockets, always irreproachably gloved and elegantly dressed, and invariably with a little piece of his white handkerchief peeping out of the pocket of his blue and gold-laced overcoat.

The first officer presented a singular contrast to Captain Anderson, and his appearance is easily described :—an active little man, with a very sunburnt skin, a black beard almost covering his face, and legs which defied every lurch of the vessel. A skilful, energetic seaman, he gave his orders in a clear, decided tone, the boatswain repeating them with a voice like the roaring of a hoarse lion. The second officer's name was W——: I think he was a naval officer, on board the "Great Eastern" by special permission; he had all the appearance of a regular "Jack-tar."

Besides the ship officers, the engines were under the command of a chief engineer, assisted by eight or ten engineering officers, and a battalion of two hundred and fifty men, some stokers, others oilers, who hardly ever left the engine-rooms.

This army of men was well occupied night and day, having ten boilers with ten furnaces and about a hundred fires to attend to.

As for the crew of the steam-ship proper, what with quartermasters, topmen, steersmen, and cabin-boys, it comprised about one hundred men, and besides these, there were two hundred stewards employed for serving the passengers.

Every man was at his post; the pilot who was to conduct the vessel out of the Mersey had been on board since the evening before. I saw also a French pilot, who was to make the passage with us, and on her return to take the steam-ship into anchorage at Brest.

"I begin to think we shall sail to-day," said I to Lieutenant H——.

THEN BEGAN THE SLOW INTERMINABLE ASCENT.

"We are only waiting for our passengers," replied my countryman.

"Are there many?"

"Twelve or thirteen hundred."

At half-past eleven the tender was hailed, laden with passengers, who, as I afterwards learnt, were Californians, Canadians, Americans, Peruvians, English, Germans, and two or three Frenchmen. Among the most distinguished were the celebrated Cyrus Field of New York, the Honourable John Rose of Canada, the Honourable J. Mac Alpine of New York, Mr. and Mrs. Alfred Cohen of San Francisco, Mr. and Mrs. Whitney of Montreal, Captain Mc Ph—— and his wife. Among the French was the founder of the "Great Eastern Freight Company," M. Jules D——, representative of the "Telegraph Construction and Maintenance Company," who had made a contribution of twenty thousand pounds to the fund.

The tender ranged herself at the foot of a flight of steps, and then began the slow, interminable ascent of passengers and luggage.

The first care of each passenger, when he had once set foot on the steamer, was to go and secure his place in the dining-room; his card, or his name written on a scrap of paper, was enough to insure his possession.

I remained on deck in order to notice all the details of

embarkation. At half-past twelve the luggage was all on board, and I saw thousands of packages of every description, from chests large enough to contain a suite of furniture, to elegant little travelling-cases and fanciful American and English trunks, heaped together pell-mell. All these were soon cleared from the deck, and stowed away in the store-rooms; workmen and porters returned to the tender, which steered off, after having blackened the side of the "Great Eastern" with her smoke.

I was going back towards the bows, when suddenly I found myself face to face with the young man I had seen on Prince's Landing-Stage. He stopped on seeing me, and held out his hand, which I warmly shook.

"You, Fabian!" I cried.   "You here?"

"Even so, my dear friend."

"I was not mistaken, then; it was really you I saw on the quay a day or two since."

"It is most likely," replied Fabian, "but I did not see you."

"And you are going to America?"

"Certainly! Do you think I could spend a month's leave better than in travelling?"

"How fortunate that you thought of making your tour in the 'Great Eastern'!"

"It was not chance at all, my dear fellow. I read in the newspaper that you were one of the passengers; and as we have not met for some years now, I came on board, in order to make the passage with you."

" Have you come from India ?"

"Yes, by the 'Godavery,' which arrived at Liverpool the day before yesterday."

"And you are travelling, Fabian ?" I asked, noticing his pale, sad face.

"To divert my mind, if I can," interrupted Captain Mac Elwin, warmly pressing my hand.

CHAPTER IV.

FABIAN left me, to look for his cabin, which, according to the ticket he held in his hand, was number seventy-three of the grand saloon series. At this moment large volumes of smoke curled from the chimneys; the steam hissed with a deafening noise through the escape-pipes, and fell in a fine rain over the deck; a noisy eddying of water announced that the engines were at work. We were at last going to start,

First of all the anchor had to be raised. The "Great Eastern" swung round with the tide; all was now clear, and Captain Anderson was obliged to choose this moment to set sail, for the width of the "Great Eastern" did not allow of her turning round in the Mersey. He was more master of his ship and more certain of guiding her skilfully in the midst of the numerous boats always plying on the river when stemming the rapid current than when driven by the ebb-tide; the least collision with this gigantic body would have proved disastrous.

To weigh anchor under these circumstances required considerable exertion, for the pressure of the tide stretched the chains by which the ship was moored, and besides this, a strong south-wester blew with full force on her hull, so that it required powerful engines to hoist the heavy anchors from their muddy beds. An anchor-boat, intended for this purpose, had just stoppered on the chains, but the windlasses were not sufficiently powerful, and they were obliged to use the steam apparatus which the "Great Eastern" had at her disposal.

At the bows was an engine of sixty-six horse-power. In order to raise the anchors it was only necessary to send the steam from the boilers into its cylinders to obtain immediately a considerable power, which could be directly applied to the windlass on which the chains were fastened. This was done ; but powerful as it was, this engine was found insufficient, and fifty of the crew were set to turn the capstan with bars, thus the anchors were gradually drawn in, but it was slow work.

I was on the poop at the bows with several other passengers at this moment, watching the details of departure. Near me stood a traveller, who frequently shrugged his shoulders impatiently, and did not spare disparaging jokes on the tardiness of the work. He was a thin, nervous little man, with quick, restless eyes : a physiognomist could easily see that the things of this life always appeared on their funny side to this philosopher of Democrates school, for his risible muscles were never still for a moment; but without describing him further, I need only say I found him a very pleasant fellow-traveller.

"I thought until now, sir," said he to me, "that engines were made to help men, not men to help engines."

I was going to reply to this wise observation, when there was a loud cry, and immediately my companion and I were hurled towards the bows ; every man at the capstan-bars was knocked down; some got up again, others lay scattered on the deck. A catch had broken, and the capstan being forced round by the frightful pressure of the chains, the men, caught by the rebound, were struck violently on the head and chest. Freed from their broken rope-bands, the capstan-bars flew in all directions like grape-shot, killing four sailors, and wounding twelve others ; among the latter was the boatswain, a Scotchman from Dundee.

The spectators hurried towards the unfortunate men, the wounded were taken to the hospital at the stern ; as for the four already dead, preparations were immediately made to send them on shore: so lightly do Anglo-Saxons regard death, that this event made very little impression on board. These unhappy men, killed and wounded, were only tools, which could be replaced at very little expense. The tender, already some distance off, was hailed, and in a few minutes she was alongside.

I went towards the fore-part of the vessel, the staircase had not yet been raised. The four corpses, enveloped in coverings, were let down, and placed on the deck of the tender. One of the surgeons on board embarked to go with them to Liverpool, with injunctions to rejoin the "Great Eastern" as quickly as possible. The tender immediately sheered off, and the sailors went to the bows, to wash the stains of blood from the deck.

I ought to add that one of the passengers, slightly wounded by the breaking of the pinion, took advantage of this circumstance to leave by the tender; he had already had enough of the "Great Eastern."

I watched the little boat going off full steam, and, turning round, I heard my ironical fellow-traveller mutter,—

"A good beginning for a voyage!"

"A very bad one, sir," said I. "To whom have I the honour of speaking?"

"To Dr. Dean Pitferge."

CHAPTER V.

THE work of weighing anchors was resumed; with the help of the anchor-boat the chains were eased, and the anchors at last left their tenacious depths. A quarter past one sounded from the Birkenhead clock-towers, the moment of departure could not be deferred, if it was intended to make use of the tide. The captain and pilot went on the foot-bridge; one lieutenant placed himself near the screw-signal apparatus, another near that of the paddle-wheel, in case of the failure of the steam-engine; four other steersmen watched at the stern, ready to put in action the great wheels placed on the gratings of the hatchings. The "Great Eastern," making head against the current, was now only waiting to descend the river with the ebb-tide.

The order for departure was given, the paddles slowly struck the water, the screw bubbled at the stern, and the enormous vessel began to move.

The greater part of the passengers on the poop were

gazing at the double landscape of Liverpool and Birken-head, studded with manufactory chimneys. The Mersey, covered with ships, some lying at anchor, others ascending and descending the river, offered only a winding passage for our steam ship. But under the hand of a pilot, sensible to the least inclinations of her rudder, she glided through the narrow passages, like a whale-boat beneath the oar of a vigorous steersman. At one time I thought that we were going to run foul of a brig, which was drifting across the stream, her bows nearly grazing the hull of the "Great Eastern," but a collision was avoided, and when from the height of the upper deck I looked at this ship, which was not of less than seven or eight hundred tons burden, she seemed to me no larger than the tiny boats which children play with on the lakes of Regent's Park or the Serpentine. It was not long before the "Great Eastern" was opposite the Liverpool landing-stages, but the four cannons which were to have saluted the town, were silent out of respect to the dead, for the tender was disembarking them at this moment; however, loud hurrahs replaced the reports which are the last expressions of national politeness. Immediately there was a vigorous clapping of hands and waving of handkerchiefs, with all the enthusiasm with which the English hail the departure of every vessel, be it only a simple yacht sailing round a bay. But with what shouts they were answered ! what echoes they called forth from the quays! There were thousands of spectators on both the Liverpool and Birkenhead sides, and boats laden with sight-seers swarmed on the Mersey. The sailors manning the yards of the "Lord Clyde," lying at anchor opposite the docks, saluted the giant with their hearty cheers.

But even the noise of the cheering could not drown the frightful discord of several bands playing at the same time. Flags were incessantly hoisted in honour of the "Great Eastern," but soon the cries grew faint in the distance. Our steam-ship ranged near the "Tripoli," a Cunard emigrant-boat, which in spite of her 2000 tons burden looked like a mere barge; then the houses grew fewer and more scattered on both shores, the landscape was no longer blackened with smoke; and brick walls, with the exception of some long regular buildings intended for workmen's houses, gave way to the open country, with pretty villas dotted here and there. Our last salutation reached us from the platform of the lighthouse and the walls of the bastion.

At three o'clock the "Great Eastern" had crossed the bar of the Mersey, and shaped her course down St. George's Channel. There was a strong sou'wester blowing, and a heavy swell on the sea, but the steam-ship did not feel it.

Towards four o'clock the Captain gave orders to heave

EVERY MAN AT THE CAPSTAN BARS WAS KNOCKED DOWN.

Page 42

to ; the tender put on full steam to rejoin us, as she was bringing back the doctor. When the boat came alongside a rope-ladder was thrown out, by which he ascended, not without some difficulty. Our more agile pilot slid down by the same way into his boat, which was awaiting him, each rower provided with a cork jacket. Some minutes after he went on board a charming little schooner waiting to catch the breeze.

Our course was immediately continued ; under the pressure of the paddles and the screw, the speed of the "Great Eastern" greatly increased ; in spite of the wind ahead, she neither rolled nor pitched. Soon the shades of night stretched across the sea, and Holyhead Point was lost in the darkness.

CHAPTER VI.

THE next day, the 27th of March, the "Great Eastern" coasted along the deeply-indented Irish shore. I had chosen my cabin at the bows; it was a small room well lighted by two skylights. A second row of cabins separated it from the first saloon, so that neither the noise of conversation, nor the rattling of pianos, which were not wanting on board, could reach me. It was an isolated cabin ; the furniture consisted of a sofa, a bedstead, and a toilet-table.

The next morning at seven o'clock, having crossed the first two rooms, I went on deck. A few passengers were already pacing the upper decks ; an almost imperceptible swell balanced the steamer ; the wind, however, was high, but the sea, protected by the coast, was comparatively calm.

From the poop of the smoking-room, I perceived that long line of shore, the continual verdure of which has won for it the name of "Emerald Coast." A few solitary

SOON WE CAME IN SIGHT OF QUEENSTOWN.

Page 29.

houses, a string of tide-waiters, a wreath of white smoke curling from between two hills, indicating the passing of a train, an isolated signal-post making grimacing gestures to the vessels at large, here and there animated the scene.

The sea between us and the coast was of a dull green shade; there was a fresh breeze blowing, mists floated above the water like spray. Numerous vessels, brigs and schooners, were awaiting the tide; steamers puffing away their black smoke were soon distanced by the "Great Eastern," although she was going at a very moderate speed.

Soon we came in sight of Queenstown, a small "calling-place," before which several fishermen's boats were at work. It is here that all ships bound for Liverpool, whether steamers or sailing-ships, throw out their despatch-bags, which are carried to Dublin in a few hours by an express train always in readiness. From Dublin they are conveyed across the channel to Holy-head by a fast steamer, so that despatches thus sent are one day in advance of the most rapid Transatlantic steamers.

About nine o'clock the bearings of the "Great Eastern" were west-north-west. I was just going on deck, when I met Captain Mac Elwin, accompanied by a friend, a tall, robust man, with a light beard and long moustache which mingled with the whiskers and left the chin bare, after the fashion of the day. This tall fellow was the exact type of an English officer; his figure was erect without stiffness, his look calm, his walk dignified but easy; his whole appearance seemed to indicate unusual courage, and I was not mistaken in him.

"My friend, Archibald Corsican," said Fabian to me, "a captain in the 22nd regiment of the Indian army, like myself."

Thus introduced, Captain Corsican and I bowed.

"We hardly saw each other yesterday, Fabian," said I, shaking Captain Mac Elwin's hand, "we were in the bustle of departure, so that all I know about you is that it was not chance which brought you on board the 'Great Eastern.' I must confess that if I have anything to do with your decision—"

"Undoubtedly, my dear fellow," interrupted Fabian; " Captain Corsican and I came to Liverpool with the intention of taking our berths on board the 'China,' a Cunard steamer, when we heard that the 'Great Eastern' was going to attempt another passage from England to America; it was a chance we might not get again, and learning that you were on board I did not hesitate, as I had not seen you since we took that delightful trip in the Scandinavian States three years ago; so now you know how it was that the tender brought us here yesterday."

CAPTAIN CORSICAN AND I BOWED

Page 40

"My dear Fabian," I replied, "I believe that neither Captain Corsican nor yourself will regret your decision, as a passage across the Atlantic in this huge boat cannot fail to be interesting even to you who are so little used to the sea. But now let us talk about yourself. Your last letter, and it is not more than six weeks since I received it, bore the Bombay post-mark, so that I was justified in believing you were still with your regiment."

"We were so three weeks ago," said Fabian, "leading the half-military, half-country life of Indian officers, employing most of our time in hunting; my friend here is a famed tiger-killer; however, as we are both single and without family ties, we thought we would let the poor wild beasts of the peninsula rest for a time, while we came to Europe to breathe a little of our native air. We obtained a year's leave, and travelling by way of the Red Sea, Suez, and France, we reached Old England with the utmost possible speed."

" Old England," said Captain Corsican, smiling ; "we are there no longer, Fabian ; we are on board an English ship, but it is freighted by a French company, and it is taking us to America ; three different flags float over our heads, signifying that we are treading on Franco-Anglo-American boards."

"What does it matter," replied Fabian, and a painful expression passed over his face ; "what does it matter, so

long as it whiles away the time? 'Movement is life;' and
it is well to be able to forget the past, and kill the present
by continual change. In a few days I shall be at New
York, where I hope to meet again my sister and her children,
whom I have not seen for several years ; then we shall visit
the great lakes, and descend the Mississippi as far as
New Orleans, where we shall look for sport on the Amazon.
From America we are going to Africa, where the lions and
elephants will make the Cape their 'rendezvous,' in order
to celebrate the arrival of Captain Corsican. Finally, we
shall return and impose on the Sepoys the caprices of the
metropolis."

Fabian spoke with a nervous volubility, and his breast
heaved ; evidently there was some great grief weighing on
his mind, the cause of which I was as yet ignorant of, but
with which Archibald seemed to be well acquainted. He
evinced a warm friendship for Fabian, who was several years
younger than himself, treating him like a younger brother,
with a devotion which at times almost amounted to
heroism.

At this moment our conversation was interrupted by the
sound of a horn, which announced the half-past twelve
lunch. Four times a day, to the great satisfaction of the
passengers, this shrill horn sounded : at half-past eight
for breakfast, half-past twelve for lunch, four o'clock for
dinner, and at seven for tea. In a few minutes the long

streets were deserted, and soon the tables in the immense saloons were filled with guests. I succeeded in getting a place near Fabian and Captain Corsican.

The dining-rooms were provided with four long rows of tables ; the glasses and bottles placed in swing-racks kept perfectly steady ; the roll of the steamer was almost imperceptible, so that the guests—men, women, and children— could eat their lunch without any fear. Numerous waiters were busy carrying round the tastily-arranged dishes, and supplying the demands for wine and beer ; the Californians certainly distinguished themselves by their proclivities for champagne. Near her husband sat an old laundress, who had found gold in the San Francisco washing-tubs, emptying a bottle of champagne in no time ; two or three pale, delicate-looking young ladies were eagerly devouring slices of red beef ; and others discussing with evident satisfaction the merits of rhubarb tart, &c. Every one worked away in the highest spirits ; one could have fancied oneself at a restaurant in the middle of Paris instead of the open sea.

Lunch over, the decks were again filled ; people bowed and spoke to each other in passing as formally as if they were walking in Hyde Park ; children played and ran about, throwing their balls and bowling hoops as they might have done on the gravel walks of the Tuileries ; the greater part of the men walked up and down smoking ; the ladies, seated on folding-chairs, worked, read, or talked together, whilst the governesses and nurses looked after the children. A few corpulent Americans swung themselves backwards and for- wards in their rocking-chairs; the ship's officers were con- tinually passing to and fro, some going to their watch on the bridge, others answering the absurd questions put to them by some of the passengers; whilst the tones of an organ and two or three pianos making a distracting discord, reached us through the lulls in the wind.

About three o'clock a loud shouting was heard; the passengers crowded on to the poop; the " Great Eastern " had ranged within two cable-lengths of a vessel which she had overhauled. It was the " Propontis," on her way to New York, which was saluting the giant of the seas on her passage, which compliment the giant returned.

Land was still in sight at four o'clock, but hardly dis- cernible through the mist which had suddenly surrounded us. Soon we saw the light of Fastenet Beacon, situated on an isolated rock. Night set in. during which we must have doubled Cape Clear, the most southerly point of Ireland.

CHAPTER VII.

I SAID that the length of the "Great Eastern" exceeded two hectometres. For the benefit of those partial to comparisons, I will add that it is a third longer than the " Pont des Arts;" in reality this steam-ship measures 673 feet at the load water-line, between the perpendiculars ; the upper deck is 680 feet from stem to stern ; that is to say, its length is double that of the largest transatlantic steamers ; its width amidships is about 71 feet, and behind the paddles about 107 feet.

The hull of the "Great Eastern" is proof against the most formidable seas ; it is double, and is composed of a number of cells placed between the deck and hold ; besides these, thirteen compartments, separated by water-tight partitions, increase the security against fire or the inlet of water. Ten thousand tons of iron were used in the construction of this hull, and 3,000,000 rivets secured the iron plates on her sides.

The "Great Eastern" draws 30 feet of water with a cargo of 28,500 tons, and with a light cargo, from 20 to 30 feet. She is capable of receiving 10,000 passengers, so that out of the 373 principal districts in France, 274 are less populated than this floating sub-prefecture with its average number of passengers.

The lines of the "Great Eastern" are very elongated; her straight stem is pierced with hawse-holes, through which the anchor-chains pass; no signs of dents or protuberances are to be seen on her finely-cut bows, but the slight sweep of her rounded stern somewhat mars the general effect.

From the deck rise six masts and five chimneys. The three masts in front are the "fore-gigger" and the "foremast" (both of them mizen-masts) and the "main-mast." The last three astern are the "after-main-mast," "mizen-mast," and "after-gigger." The fore-masts and the main-masts carry the schooner-sails, the top-sails, and the gallant-sails; the four other masts are only rigged with ordinary sails; the whole forming 5400 square yards of good canvas. On the spacious mastheads of the second and third masts a band of soldiers could easily manœuvre. Of these six masts, supported by shrouds and metallic back-stays, the second, third, and fourth are made of sheet-iron, and are really masterpieces of ironwork. At the base they measure 43 inches in diameter, and the largest (the

main-mast) rises to the height of 207 French feet, which is
higher than the towers of Notre Dame.

As to the chimneys, the two belonging to the paddle-
engine and the three belonging to the screw, they are
enormous cylinders, 90 feet high, supported by chains
fastened to the upper deck.

The arrangements with regard to the interior are admirable. The laundries and the crew's berths are shut
off at the fore-part, then come the ladies' saloon and a
grand saloon ornamented with lustres, swinging lamps,
and pictures. These magnificent rooms are lighted by
side sky-lights, supported on elegant-gilded pillars, and
communicate with the upper-deck by wide staircases with
metallic steps and mahogany balusters.

On deck are arranged four rows of cabins separated
by a passage, some are reached by a landing, others on
a lower story by private staircases. At the stern the
three immense dining-rooms run in the same direction as
the cabins, a passage leads from the saloons at the stern to
those at the bows round the paddle-engine, between its
sheet-iron partitions and the ship's offices.

The engines of the "Great Eastern" are justly considered as masterpieces—I was going to say of clock-
work, for there is nothing more astonishing than to
see this enormous machine working with the precision
and ease of a clock, a singular contrast to the screw,

which works rapidly and furiously, as though getting itself into a rage.

Independently of these two engines, the " Great Eastern" possesses six auxiliary ones to work the capstans, so that it is evident steam plays an important part on board.

Such is this steam-ship, without equal and known every-where; which, however, did not hinder a French captain from making this *naïve* remark in his log-book: " Passed a ship with six masts and five chimneys, supposed to be the 'Great Eastern.'"

CHAPTER VIII.

ON Wednesday night the weather was very bad, my balance was strangely variable, and I was obliged to lean with my knees and elbows against the sideboard, to prevent myself from falling. Portmanteaus and bags came in and out of my cabin; an unusual hubbub reigned in the adjoining saloon, in which two or three hundred packages were making expeditions from one end to the other, knocking the tables and chairs with loud crashes; doors slammed, the boards creaked, the partitions made that groaning noise peculiar to pine wood; bottles and glasses jingled together in their racks, and a cataract of plates and dishes rolled about on the pantry floors. I heard the irregular roaring of the screw, and the wheels beating the water, sometimes entirely immersed, and at others striking the empty air; by all these signs I concluded that the wind had freshened, and the steam-ship was no longer indifferent to the billows.

At six o'clock next morning, after passing a sleepless

night, I got up and dressed myself, as well as I could with one hand, while with the other I clutched at the sides of my cabin, for without support it was impossible to keep one's feet, and I had quite a serious struggle to get on my over-coat. I left my cabin, and helping myself with hands and feet through the billows of luggage, I crossed the saloon, scrambling up the stairs on my knees, like a Roman peasant devoutly climbing the steps of the "Scala santa" of Pontius Pilate; and at last, reaching the deck, I hung on firmly to the nearest kevel.

No land in sight; we had doubled Cape Clear in the night, and around us was that vast circumference bounded by the line, where water and sky appear to meet. The slate-coloured sea broke in great foamless billows. The "Great Eastern" struck amidships, and, supported by no sail, rolled frightfully, her bare masts describing immense circles in the air. There was no heaving to speak of, but the rolling was dreadful, it was impossible to stand upright. The officer on watch, clinging to the bridge, looked as if he was in a swing.

From kevel to kevel, I managed to reach the paddles on the starboard side, the deck was damp and slippery from the spray and mist: I was just going to fasten myself to a stanchion of the bridge when a body rolled at my feet.

It was Dr. Pitferge, my quaint friend : he scrambled on to his knees, and looking at me, said, —

WHEN A BODY ROLLED AT MY FEET.

Page 40.

"That's all right, the amplitude of the arc, described by the sides of the 'Great Eastern,' is forty degrees; that is, twenty degrees below the horizontal, and twenty above it."

"Indeed!" cried I, laughing, not at the observation, but at the circumstances under which it was made.

"Yes!" replied the Doctor. "During the oscillation the speed of the sides is fifty-nine inches per second, a transatlantic boat half the size takes but the same time to recover her equilibrium."

"Then," replied I, "since that is the case, there is an excess of stability in the 'Great Eastern.'"

"For her, yes, but not for her passengers," answered Dean Pitferge gaily, "for you see they come back to the horizontal quicker than they care for."

The Doctor, delighted with his repartee, raised himself, and holding each other up, we managed to reach a seat on the poop. Dean Pitferge had come off very well, with only a few bruises, and I congratulated him on his lucky escape, as he might have broken his neck.

"Oh, it is not over yet," said he; "there is more trouble coming."

"To us?"

"To the steamer, and consequently to me, to us, and to all the passengers."

"If you are speaking seriously, why did you come on board?"

"To see what is going to happen, for I should not be at all ill-pleased to witness a shipwreck!" replied the Doctor, looking at me knowingly.

"Is this the first time you have been on board the 'Great Eastern'?"

"No, I have already made several voyages in her, to satisfy my curiosity."

"You must not complain, then."

"I do not complain; I merely state facts, and patiently await the hour of the catastrophe."

Was the Doctor making fun of me? I did not know what to think, his small twinkling eyes looked very roguish; but I thought I would try him further.

"Doctor," I said, "I do not know on what facts your painful prognostics are founded, but allow me to remind you that the 'Great Eastern' has crossed the Atlantic twenty times, and most of her passages have been satisfactory."

"That's of no consequence; this ship is bewitched, to use a common expression, she cannot escape her fate; I know it, and therefore have no confidence in her. Remember what difficulties the engineers had to launch her; I believe even that Brunel, who built her, died from the 'effects of the operation,' as we doctors say."

"Ah, Doctor," said I, "are you inclined to be a materialist?"

"Why ask me that question?"

"Because I have noticed that many who do not believe in God believe in everything else, even in the evil eye."

"Make fun if you like, sir," replied the Doctor, "but allow me to continue my argument. The 'Great Eastern' has already ruined several companies. Built for the purpose of carrying emigrants to Australia, she has never once been there; intended to surpass the ocean steamers in speed, she even remains inferior to them."

"From this," said I, "it is to be concluded that—"

"Listen a minute," interrupted the Doctor. "Already one of her captains has been drowned, and he one of the most skilful, for he knew how to prevent this rolling by keeping the ship a little ahead of the waves."

"Ah, well!" said I, "the death of that able man is to be regretted."

"Then," continued Dean Pitferge, without noticing my incredulity, "strange stories are told about this ship; they say that a passenger who lost his way in the hold of the ship, like a pioneer in the forests of America, has never yet been found."

"Ah!" exclaimed I ironically, "there's a fact!"

"They say, also, that during the construction of the boilers an engineer was melted by mistake in the steam-box."

"Bravo!" cried I; "the melted engineer! 'È ben trovato.' Do you believe it, Doctor?"

" I believe," replied Pitferge, " I believe quite seriously that our voyage began badly, and that it will end in the same manner."

"But the 'Great Eastern' is a solid structure," I said, "and built so firmly that she is able to resist the most furious seas like a solid block."

" Solid she is, undoubtedly," resumed the doctor ; " but let her fall into the hollow of the waves, and see if she will rise again. Maybe she is a giant, but a giant whose strength is not in proportion to her size ; her engines are too feeble for her. Have you ever heard speak of her nineteenth passage from Liverpool to New York ?"

" No, Doctor."

" Well, I was on board. We left Liverpool on a Tuesday, the 10th of December ; there were numerous passengers, and all full of confidence. Everything went well so long as we were protected by the Irish coast from the billows of the open sea ; no rolling, no sea-sickness ; the next day, even, the same stability ; the passengers were delighted. On the 12th, however, the wind freshened towards morning; the "Great Eastern,' heading the waves, rolled considerably ; the passengers, men and women, disappeared into the cabins. At four o'clock the wind blew a hurricane ; the furniture began to dance ; a mirror in the saloon was broken by a blow from the head of your humble servant ; all the crockery was smashed to atoms ; there was a frightful uproar; eight shore-boats were torn from the davits in one swoop. At this moment our situation was serious; the paddle-wheel-engine had to be stopped; an enormous piece of lead, displaced by a lurch of the vessel, threatened to fall into its machinery; however, the screw continued to send us on. Soon the wheels began turning again, but very slowly; one of them had been damaged during the stoppage, and its spokes and paddles scraped the hull of the ship. The engine had to be stopped again, and we had to content ourselves with the screw. The night was fearful; the fury of the tempest was redoubled; the 'Great Eastern' had fallen into the trough of the sea and could not right herself; at break of day there was not a piece of iron-work remaining on the wheels. They hoisted a few sails in order to right the ship, but no sooner were they hoisted than they were carried away; confusion reigned everywhere; the cable-chains, torn from their beds, rolled from one side of the ship to the other; a cattle-pen was knocked in, and a cow fell into the ladies' saloon through the hatchway; another misfortune was the breaking of the rudder-chock, so that steering was no longer possible. Frightful crashes were heard; an oil tank, weighing over three tons, had broken from its fixings, and, rolling across the tween-decks, struck the sides alternately like a battering-ram. Saturday passed in the midst of a general terror, the ship in the trough of the sea all the time. Not until Sunday did the wind begin to abate, an American engineer on board then succeeded in fastening the chains on the rudder; we turned little by little, and the 'Great Eastern' righted herself. A week after we left Liverpool we reached Queenstown. Now, who knows, sir, where we shall be in a week ?"

CHAPTER IX.

IT must be confessed the Doctor's words were not very comforting, the passengers would not have heard them without shuddering. Was he joking, or did he speak seriously? Was it, indeed true, that he went with the "Great Eastern" in all her voyages, to be present at some catastrophe? Everything is possible for an eccentric, especially when he is English.

However, the "Great Eastern" continued her course, tossing like a canoe, and keeping strictly to the loxodromic line of steamers. It is well known, that on a flat surface, the nearest way from one point to another is by a straight line. On a sphere it is the curved line formed by the circumference of great circles. Ships have an interest in following this route, in order to make the shortest passage, but sailing vessels cannot pursue this track against a head-wind, so that steamers alone are able to maintain a direct course, and take the route of the great circles. This is what the "Great Eastern" did, making a little for the north-west.

The rolling never ceased, that horrible sea-sickness, at the same time contagious and epidemic, made rapid progress. Several of the passengers, with wan, pallid faces, and sunken cheeks, remained on deck, in order to breathe the fresh air, the greater part of them were furious at the unlucky steam-ship, which was conducting herself like a mere buoy, and at the freighter's advertisements, which had stated that sea-sickness was "unknown on board."

At nine o'clock in the morning an object three or four miles off was signalled from the larboard quarter. Was it a waif, the carcass of a whale, or the hull of a ship? As yet it was not distinguishable. A group of convalescent passengers stood on the upper-deck, at the bows, looking at this waif which was floating three hundred miles from the nearest land.

Meanwhile the "Great Eastern" was bearing towards the object signalled ; all opera-glasses were promptly raised, and there was no lack of conjecture. Between the Americans, and English, to whom every pretext for a wager is welcome, betting at once commenced. Among the most desperate of the betters I noticed a tall man, whose countenance struck me as one of profound duplicity. His features were stamped with a look of general hatred, which neither a physiognomist, nor physiologist could mistake ; his forehead was seamed with a deep furrow, his manner was at the same time audacious and listless,

THE WAIF WAS THE HULL OF A SHIP.

Page 49.

his eyebrows nearly meeting, partly concealed the stony eyes beneath, his shoulders were high and his chin thrust forward, in fact all the indications of insolence and knavery were united in his appearance. He spoke in loud pompous tones, while some of his worthy associates laughed at his coarse jokes. This personage pretended to recognize in the waif the carcass of a whale, and he backed his opinion by heavy stakes, which soon found ready acceptance.

These wagers, amounting to several hundred dollars, he lost every one; in fact, the waif was the hull of a ship; the steamer rapidly drew near it, and we could already see the rusty copper of her keel. It was a three-mast ship of about five or six hundred tons, deprived of her masts and rigging, and lying on one side, with broken chains hanging from her davits.

" Had this steam-ship been abandoned by her crew?" This was now the prevailing question, however no one appeared on the deck, perhaps the shipwrecked ones had taken refuge inside. I saw an object moving for several moments at the bows, but it turned out to be only the remains of the jib lashed to and fro by the wind.

The hull was quite visible at the distance of half a mile; she was a comparatively new ship, and in a perfect state of preservation; her cargo, which had been shifted by the wind, obliged her to lie along on her starboard side.

E

The "Great Eastern" drew nearer, and, passing round, gave notice of her presence by several shrill whistles ; but the waif remained silent, and unanimated ; nothing was to be seen, not even a shore-boat from the wrecked vessel was visible on the wide expanse of water.

The crew had undoubtedly had time to leave her, but could they have reached land, which was three hundred miles off ? Could a frail boat live on a sea like that which had rocked the "Great Eastern" so frightfully ? And when could this catastrophe have happened ? It was evident that the shipwreck had taken place farther west, for the wind and waves must have driven the hull far out of her course. These questions were destined to remain unanswered.

When the steam-ship came alongside the stern of the wreck, I could read distinctly the name "Lerida," but the port she belonged to was not given.

A merchant-vessel or a man-of-war would have had no hesitation in manning this hull which, undoubtedly, contained a valuable cargo, but as the "Great Eastern" was on regular service, she could not take this waif in tow for so many hundreds of miles; it was equally impossible to return and take it to the nearest port. Therefore, to the great regret of the sailors, it had to be abandoned, and it was soon a mere speck in the distance. The group of passengers dispersed, some to the saloons, others to their

cabins, and even the lunch-bell failed to awaken the slum-
berers, worn out by sea-sickness. About noon Captain
Anderson ordered sail to be hoisted, so that the ship,
better supported, did not roll so much.

CHAPTER X.

IN spite of the ship's disorderly conduct, life on board was becoming organized, for with the Anglo-Saxon nothing is more simple. The steam-boat is his street and his house for the time being; the Frenchman, on the contrary, always looks like a traveller.

When the weather was favourable, the boulevards were thronged with promenaders, who managed to maintain the perpendicular, in spite of the ship's motion, but with the peculiar gyrations of tipsy men. When the passengers did not go on deck, they remained either in their private sitting rooms or in the grand saloon, and then began the noisy discords of pianos, all played at the same time, which, however, seemed not to affect Saxon ears in the least. Among these amateurs, I noticed a tall, bony woman, who must have been a good musician, for, in order to facilitate reading her piece of music, she had marked all the notes with a number, and the piano-keys with a number corresponding, so that if it was note twenty-seven, she struck key twenty-seven, if fifty-three, key fifty-three, and so on, perfectly indifferent to the noise around her, or the sound of other pianos in the adjoining saloons, and her equanimity was not even disturbed when some disagreeable little children thumped with their fists on the unoccupied keys.

Whilst this concert was going on, a bystander would carelessly take up one of the books scattered here and there on the tables, and, having found an interesting passage, would read it aloud, whilst his audience listened good-humouredly, and complimented him with a flattering murmur of applause. Newspapers were scattered on the sofas, generally American and English, which always look old, although the pages have never been cut ; it is a very tiresome operation reading these great sheets, which take up so much room, but the fashion being to leave them uncut, so they remain. One day I had the patience to read the *New York Herald* from beginning to end under these circumstances, and judge if I was rewarded for my trouble when I turned to the column headed " Private : " " M. X. begs the pretty Miss Z——, whom he met yesterday in Twenty-fifth Street omnibus, to come to him tomorrow, at his rooms, No. 17, St. Nicholas Hotel ; he wishes to speak of marriage with her." What did the pretty Miss Z—— do? I don't even care to know.

I passed the whole of the afternoon in the grand saloon

talking, and observing what was going on about me. Conversation could not fail to be interesting, for my friend Dean Pitferge was sitting near me.

" Have you quite recovered from the effects of your tumble ?" I asked him.

" Perfectly," replied he, " but it's no go."

" What is no go ? You ?"

" No, our steam-ship; the screw boilers are not working well; we cannot get enough pressure."

" You are anxious, then, to get to New York ?"

" Not in the least, I speak as an engineer, that is all. I am very comfortable here, and shall sincerely regret leaving this collection of originals which chance has thrown together . . . for my recreation."

" Originals !" cried I, looking at the passengers who crowded the saloon ; " but all those people are very much alike."

" Nonsense ! ' exclaimed the Doctor, " one can see you have hardly looked at them, the species is the same, I allow, but in that species what a variety there is ! Just notice that group of men down there, with their easy-going air, their legs stretched on the sofas, and hats screwed down on their heads. They are Yankees, pure Yankees, from the small states of Maine, Vermont, and Connecticut, the produce of New England. Energetic and intelligent men, rather too much influenced by ' the

Reverends,' and who have the disagreeable fault of never putting their hands before their mouths when they sneeze. Ah! my dear sir, they are true Saxons, always keenly alive to a bargain; put two Yankees in a room together, and in an hour they will each have gained ten dollars from the other."

" I will not ask how," replied I, smiling at the Doctor, "but among them I see a little man with a consequential air, looking like a weather-cock, and dressed in a long overcoat, with rather short black trousers,—who is that gentleman?"

" He is a Protestant minister, a man of 'importance' in Massachusetts, where he is going to join his wife, an ex-governess advantageously implicated in a celebrated law-suit."

" And that tall, gloomy-looking fellow, who seems to be absorbed in calculation?"

" That man calculates: in fact," said the Doctor, " he is for ever calculating."

" Problems?"

" No, his fortune, he is a man of 'importance,' at any moment he knows almost to a farthing what he is worth; he is rich, a fourth part of New York is built on his land; a quarter of an hour ago he possessed 1,625,367 dollars and a half, but now he has only 1,625,367 dollars and a quarter"

" How came this difference in his fortune ?"

" Well! he has just smoked a quarter-dollar cigar."

Doctor Dean Pitferge amused me with his clever repartees, so I pointed out to him another group stowed away in a corner of the saloon.

"They," said he, "are people from the Far West, the tallest, who looks like a head clerk, is a man of 'importance,' the head of a Chicago bank, he always carries an album under his arm, with the principal views of his beloved city. He is, and has reason to be, proud of a city founded in a desert in 1836, which at the present day has a population of more than 400,000 souls. Near him you see a Californian couple, the young wife is delicate and charming, her well-polished husband was once a plough-boy, who one fine day turned up some nuggets. That gentleman—"

" Is a man of 'importance,   said I.

" Undoubtedly," replied the Doctor, "for his assets count by the million."

" And pray who may this tall individual be, who moves his head backwards and forwards like the pendulum of a clock ?"

" That person," replied the Doctor, " is the celebrated Cockburn of Rochester, the universal statician, who has weighed, measured, proportioned, and calculated every-thing. Question this harmless maniac, he will tell you

"THEY," SAID HE "ARE PEOPLE FROM THE FAR WEST."

Page 16.

how much bread a man of fifty has eaten in his life, and
how many cubic feet of air he has breathed. He will tell
you how many volumes in quarto the words of a Temple
lawyer would fill, and how many miles the postman
goes daily carrying nothing but love-letters; he will tell
you the number of widows who pass in one hour over
London Bridge, and what would be the height of a pile of
sandwiches consumed by the citizens of the Union in a
year; he will tell you—"

The Doctor, in his excitement, would have continued for
a long time in this strain, but other passengers passing us
were attracted by the inexhaustible stock of his original
remarks. What different characters there were in this
crowd of passengers! not one idler, however, for one does
not go from one continent to the other without some
serious motive. The most part of them were undoubtedly
going to seek their fortunes on American ground, forgetting that at twenty years of age a Yankee has made
his fortune, and that at twenty-five he is already too old to
begin the struggle.

Among these adventurers, inventors, and fortune-hunters,
Dean Pitferge pointed out to me some singularly interesting characters. Here was a chemist, a rival of Dr. Liebig,
who pretended to have discovered the art of condensing all
the nutritious parts of a cow into a meat-tablet, no larger
than a five-shilling piece. He was going to coin money

out of the cattle of the Pampas. Another, the inventor of a portable motive-power—a steam horse in a watch-case—was going to exhibit his patent in New England. Another, a Frenchman from the "Rue Chapon," was carrying to America 30,000 cardboard dolls, which said "papa" with a very successful Yankee accent, and he had no doubt but that his fortune was made.

But besides these originals, there were still others whose secrets we could not guess; perhaps among them was some cashier flying from his empty cash-box, and a detective making friends with him, only waiting for the end of the passage to take him by the collar; perhaps also we might have found in this crowd clever genii, who always find people ready to believe in them, even when they advocate the affairs of " The Oceanic Company for lighting Polynesia with gas," or " The Royal Society for making incombustible coal."

But at this moment my attention was attracted by the entrance of a young couple who seemed to be under the influence of a precocious weariness.

" They are Peruvians, my dear sir," said the Doctor, " a couple married a year ago, who have been to all parts of the world for their honeymoon. They adored each other in Japan, loved in Australia, bore with one another in India, bored each other in France, quarrelled in England, and will undoubtedly separate in America."

"And," said I, "who is that tall, haughty-looking man just coming in? from his appearance I should take him for an officer."

"He is a Mormon," replied the doctor, "an elder, Mr. Hatch, one of the great preachers in the city of Saints, What a fine type of manhood he is! Look at his proud eye, his noble countenance, and dignified bearing, so different from the Yankee. Mr. Hatch is returning from Germany and England, where he has preached Mormonism with great success, for there are numbers of this sect in Europe, who are allowed to conform to the laws of their country."

"Indeed!" said I; "I quite thought that polygamy was forbidden them in Europe."

"Undoubtedly, my dear sir, but do not think that polygamy is obligatory on Mormons; Brigham Young has his harem, because it suits him, but all his followers do not imitate him, not even those dwelling on the banks of the Salt Lake."

"Indeed! and Mr. Hatch?"

"Mr. Hatch has only one wife, and he finds that quite enough; besides, he proposes to explain his system in a meeting that he will hold one of these evenings."

"The saloon will be filled."

"Yes," said Pitferge, "if the gambling does not attract too many of the audience; you know that they play in a room at the bows? There is an Englishman there with an evil, disagreeable face, who seems to take the lead among them, he is a bad man, with a detestable reputation. Have you noticed him?"

From the Doctor's description, I had no doubt but that he was the same man who that morning had made himself conspicuous by his foolish wagers with regard to the waif. My opinion of him was not wrong. Dean Pitferge told me his name was Harry Drake, and that he was the son of a merchant at Calcutta, a gambler, a dissolute character, a duellist, and now that he was almost ruined, he was most likely going to America to try a life of adventures. "Such people," added the Doctor, "always find followers willing to flatter them, and this fellow has already formed his circle of scamps, of which he is the centre. Among them I have noticed a little short man, with a round face, a turned-up nose, wearing gold spectacles, and having the appearance of a German Jew; he calls himself a doctor, on the way to Quebec; but I take him for a low actor and one of Drake's admirers."

At this moment Dean Pitferge, who easily skipped from one subject to another, nudged my elbow. I turned my head towards the saloon door: a young man about twenty-eight, and a girl of seventeen, were coming in arm in arm.

"A newly-married pair?" asked I.

"No," replied the Doctor, in a softened tone, "an engaged

I OFTEN SEE THEM LEANING OVER THE RAILINGS OF THE ENGINE-
ROOM.

Page 61.

couple, who are only waiting for their arrival in New York to get married, they have just made the tour of Europe, of course with their family's consent, and they know now that they are made for one another. Nice young people ; it is a pleasure to look at them. I often see them leaning over the railings of the engine-rooms, counting the turns of the wheels, which do not go half fast enough for their liking. Ah! sir, if our boilers were heated like those two youthful hearts, see how our speed would increase!"

CHAPTER XI.

THIS day, at half-past twelve, a steersman posted up on the grand saloon door the following observation :—

Lat. 51° 15′ N.

Long. 18° 13′ W.

Dist. : Fastenet, 323 miles.

This signified that at noon we were three hundred and twenty-three miles from the Fastenet lighthouse, the last which we had passed on the Irish coast, and at 51° 15′ north latitude, and 18° 13′ west longitude, from the meridian of Greenwich. It was the ship's bearing, which the captain thus made known to the passengers every day. By consulting this bearing, and referring it to a chart, the course of the " Great Eastern " might be followed. Up to this time she had only made three hundred and twenty miles in thirty-six hours, it was not satisfactory, for a steamer at its ordinary speed does not go less than three hundred miles in twenty-four hours.

After having left the Doctor, I spent the rest of the day with Fabian; we had gone to the stern, which Pitferge called "walking in the country." There alone, and leaning over the taffrail, we surveyed the great expanse of water, while around us rose the briny vapours distilled from the spray; small rainbows, formed by the refraction of the sun's rays, spanned the foaming waves. Below us, at a distance of forty feet, the screw was beating the water with a tremendous force, making its copper gleam in the midst of what appeared to be a vast conglomeration of liquefied emeralds, the fleecy track extending as far as the eye could reach, mingled in a milky path the foam from the screw, and the paddle engines, whilst the white and black fringed plumage of the sea-gulls flying above, cast rapid shadows over the sea.

Fabian was looking at the magic of the waves without speaking. What did he see in this liquid mirror, which gave scope to the most capricious flights of imagination? Was some vanished face passing before his eyes, and bidding him a last farewell? Did he see a drowning shadow in these eddying waters? He seemed to me sadder than usual, and I dared not ask him the cause of his grief.

After the long separation which had estranged us from each other, it was for him to confide in me, and for me to await his confidences. He had told me as much of his past life as he wished me to know; his life in the Indian garrison, his hunting, and adventures; but not a word had he said of the emotions which swelled in his heart, or the cause of the sighs which heaved his breast ; undoubtedly Fabian was not one who tried to lessen his grief by speaking of it, and therefore he suffered the more.

Thus we remained leaning over the sea, and as I turned my head I saw the great paddles emerging under the regular action of the engine.

Once Fabian said to me, "This track is indeed magnificent. One would think that the waves were amusing themselves with tracing letters ! Look at the ' l's' and 'e's'. Am I deceived ?   No, they are indeed always the same letters."

Fabian's excited imagination saw in these eddyings that which it wished to see.   But what could these letters signify ? What remembrance did they call forth in Fabian's mind ? The latter had resumed his silent contemplation, when suddenly he said to me, —

" Come to me, come ; that gulf will draw me in ! "

" What is the matter with you, Fabian," said I, taking him by both hands ; " what is the matter, my friend ?"

" I have here," said he, pressing his hand on his heart, " I have here a disease which will kill me."

" A disease ?" said I to him, " a disease with no hope of cure ? "

" No hope."

And without another word Fabian went to the saloon, and then on to his cabin.

CHAPTER XII.

THE next day, Saturday, 30th of March, the weather was fine, and the sea calm ; our progress was more rapid, and the "Great Eastern" was now going at the rate of twelve knots an hour.

The wind had set south, and the first officer ordered the mizen and the top-mast sails to be hoisted, so that the ship was perfectly steady. Under this fine sunny sky the upper decks again became crowded ; ladies appeared in fresh costumes, some walking about, others sitting down— I was going to say on the grass-plats beneath the shady trees, and the children resumed their interrupted games. With a few soldiers in uniform, strutting about with their hands in their pockets, one might have fancied oneself on a French promenade.

At noon, the weather being favourable, Captain Anderson and two officers went on to the bridge, in order to take the sun's altitude ; each held a sextant in his hand, and from

F

time to time scanned the southern horizon, towards which their horizon-glasses were inclined.

"Noon," exclaimed the Captain, after a short time.

Immediately a steersman rang a bell on the bridge, and all the watches on board were regulated by the statement which had just been made.

Half-an-hour later, the following observation was posted up :—

> Lat. 51° 10′ N.
> Long. 24° 13′ W.
> Course, 227 miles. Distance 550.

We had thus made two hundred and twenty-seven miles since noon the day before.

I did not see Fabian once during the day. Several times, uneasy about his absence, I passed his cabin, and was convinced that he had not left it.

He must have wished to avoid the crowd on deck, and evidently sought to isolate himself from this tumult. I met Captain Corsican, and for an hour we walked on the poop. He often spoke of Fabian, and I could not help telling him what had passed between Fabian and myself the evening before.

"Yes," said Captain Corsican, with an emotion he did not try to disguise. "Two years ago Fabian had the right to think himself the happiest of men, and now he is the most unhappy." Archibald Corsican told me, in a few words, th⸱⸱

at Bombay Fabian had known a charming young girl, a Miss Hodges. He loved her, and was beloved by her. Nothing seemed to hinder a marriage between Miss Hodges and Captain Mac Elwin ; when, by her father's consent, the young girl's hand was sought by the son of a merchant at Calcutta. It was an old business affair, and Hodges, a harsh, obstinate, and unfeeling man, who happened at this time to be in a delicate position with his Calcutta correspondent, thinking that the marriage would settle everything well, sacrificed his daughter to the interests of his fortune. The poor child could not resist ; they put her hand into that of the man she did not and could not love, and who, from all appearance, had no love for her. It was a mere business transaction, and a barbarous deed. The husband carried off his wife the day after they were married, and since then Fabian has never seen her whom he has always loved.

This story showed me clearly that the grief which seemed to oppress Fabian was indeed serious.

"What was the young girl's name?" asked I of Captain Corsican.

"Ellen Hodges," replied he.

"Ellen,—that name explains the letters which Fabian thought he saw yesterday in the ship's track. And what is the name of this poor young woman's husband? said I to the Captain.

"Harry Drake."

"Drake!" cried I, "but that man is on board."

" He here!" exclaimed Corsican, seizing my hand, and looking straight at me.

"Yes," I replied, "he is on board."

"Heaven grant that they may not meet!" said the Captain gravely. "Happily they do not know each other, at least Fabian does not know Harry Drake; but that name uttered in his hearing would be enough to cause an outburst."

I then related to Captain Corsican what I knew of Harry Drake, that is to say, what Dr. Dean Pitferge had told me of him. I described him such as he was, an insolent, noisy adventurer, already ruined by gambling, and other vices, and ready to do anything to get money; at this moment Harry Drake passed close to us; I pointed him out to the Captain, whose eyes suddenly grew animated, and he made an angry gesture, which I arrested.

"Yes," said he, "there is the face of a villain. But where is he going?"

"To America, they say, to try and get by chance what he does not care to work for."

"Poor Ellen!" murmured the Captain; "where is she now?"

"Perhaps this wretch has abandoned her, or why should she not be on board?" said Corsican, looking at me.

This idea crossed my mind for the first time, but I re-

FERAT

"PRAIN

HE MADE AN ANGRY GESTURE WHICH I ARRESTED.

Page 94.

jected it. No ; Ellen was not, could not be on board ; she could not have escaped Dr. Pitferge's inquisitive eye. No! she cannot have accompanied Drake on this voyage !

"May what you say be true, sir!" replied Captain Corsican ; "for the sight of that poor victim reduced to so much misery would be a terrible blow to Fabian : I do not know what would happen, for Fabian is a man who would kill Drake like a dog. I ask you, as a proof of your friendship, never to lose sight of him ; so that if anything should happen, one of us may be near, to throw ourselves between him and his enemy. You understand a duel must not take place between these two men. Alas ! neither here nor elsewhere. A woman cannot marry her husband's murderer, however unworthy that husband may have been."

I well understood Captain Corsican's reason. Fabian could not be his own justiciary. It was foreseeing, from a distance, coming events, but how is it that the uncertainty of human things is so little taken into account ? A presentiment was boding in my mind. Could it be possible, that in this common life on board, in this every-day mingling together, that Drake's noisy personality could remain unnoticed by Fabian ? An accident, a trifle, a mere name uttered, would it not bring them face to face ? Ah! how I longed to hasten the speed of the steamer which carried them both ! Before leaving Captain Corsican I promised to keep a watch on our friend, and to observe Drake, whom on his part he engaged not to lose sight of; then he shook my hand, and we parted.

Towards evening a dense mist swept over the ocean, and the darkness was intense. The brilliantly-lighted saloons contrasted singularly with the blackness of the night. Waltzes and ballad 'songs followed each other; all received with frantic applause, and even hurrahs were not wanting, when the actor from T——, sitting at the piano, bawled his songs with the self-possession of a strolling player.

CHAPTER XIII.

THE next day, the 31st of March, was Sunday. How would this day be kept on board? Would it be the English or American Sunday, which closes the "bars" and the "taps" during service hours; which withholds the butcher's hand from his victim; which keeps the baker's shovel from the oven; which causes a suspension of business; extinguishes the fires of the manufactories; which closes the shops, opens the churches, and moderates the speed of the railway trains, contrary to the customs in France? Yes, it must be kept thus, or almost thus.

First of all, during the service, although the weather was fine, and we might have gained some knots, the Captain did not order the sails to be hoisted, as it would have been "improper." I thought myself very fortunate that the screw was allowed to continue its work, and when I inquired of a fierce Puritan the reason for this tolerance, " Sir," said he to me, " that which comes directly from God

must be respected ; the wind is in His hand, the steam is
in the power of man."

I was willing to content myself with this reason, and in
the meantime observed what was going on on board.

All the crew were in full uniform, and dressed with extreme propriety. I should not have been surprised to see
the stokers working in black clothes ; the officers and
engineers wore their finest uniforms, with gilt buttons ;
their shoes shone with a British lustre, and rivalled their
glazed hats with an intense irradiation. All these good
people seemed to have hats and boots of a dazzling bright-
ness. The Captain and the first officer set the example,
and with new gloves and military attire, glittering and per-
fumed, they paced up and down the bridges awaiting the
hour for service.

The sea was magnificent and resplendent beneath the
first rays of a spring sun ; not a sail in sight. The "Great
Eastern" occupied alone the centre of the immense·ex-
panse. At ten o'clock the bell on deck tolled slowly and at
regular intervals ; the ringer, who was a steersman, dressed
in his best, managed to obtain from this bell a kind of solemn,
religious tone, instead of the metallic peals with which
it accompanied the whistling of the boilers, when the ship
was surrounded by fog. Involuntarily one looked for the
village steeple which was calling to prayer.

At this moment numerous groups appeared at the doors

of the cabins, at the bows and stern ; the boulevards were soon filled with men, women, and children carefully dressed for the occasion. Friends exchanged quiet greetings ; every one held a Prayer-book in his hand, and all were waiting for the last bell which would announce the beginning of service. I saw also piles of Bibles, which were to be distributed in the church, heaped upon trays generally used for sandwiches.

The church was the great saloon, formed by the upperdeck at the stern, the exterior of which, from its width and regularity of structure, reminded one very much of the hotel of the Ministère des Finances, in the Rue de Rivoli. I entered. Numbers of the faithful were already in their places. A profound silence reigned among the congregation ; the officers occupied the apsis of the church, and, in the midst of them, stood Captain Anderson, as pastor. My friend Dean Pitferge was near him, his quick little eyes running over the whole assembly. I will venture to say he was there more out of curiosity than anything else.

At half-past ten the Captain rose, and the service began ; he read a chapter from the Old Testament. After each verse the congregation murmured the one following ; the shrill soprano voices of the women and children distinctly separate from the baritone of the men. This Biblical dialogue lasted for about half-an-hour, and the simple, at the same time impressive ceremony, was performed with a

puritanical gravity. Captain Anderson assuming the office
of pastor on board, in the midst of the vast ocean, and
speaking to a crowd of listeners, hanging, as it were, over
the verge of an abyss, claimed the respect and attention of
the most indifferent. It would have been well if the service
had concluded with the reading; but when the Captain
had finished a speaker arose, who could not fail to arouse
feelings of violence and rebellion where tolerance and
meditation should reign.

It was the reverend gentleman of whom I have before
spoken—a little, fidgety man, an intriguing Yankee; one
of those ministers who exercise such a powerful influence
over the States of New England. His sermon was already
prepared, the occasion was good, and he intended to make
use of it. Would not the good Yorrick have done the
same? I looked at Dean Pitferge; the Doctor did not
frown, but seemed inclined to try the preacher's zeal.

The latter gravely buttoned his black overcoat, placed
his silk cap on the table, drew out his handkerchief, with
which he touched his lips lightly, and taking in the assembly
at a glance—

"In the beginning," said he, "God created America, and
rested on the seventh day." . . . . . .

Thereupon I reached the door.

CHAPTER XIV.

AT lunch Dean Pitferge told me that the reverend gentleman had admirably enlarged on his text. Battering rams,
armed forts, and submarine torpedoes had figured in his
discourse ; as for himself, he was made great by the great-
ness of America. If it pleases America to be thus extolled,
I have nothing to say.

Entering the grand saloon, I read the following note :—

Lat. 50° 8′ N.

Long. 30° 44′ W.

Course, 255 miles.

Always the same result. We had only made eleven
hundred miles, including the three hundred and ten
between Fastenet and Liverpool, about a third part of our
voyage. During the remainder of the day officers, sailors,
and passengers continued to rest in accordance with established custom. Not a piano sounded in the silent saloons ;
the chess-men did not leave their box, or the cards their
case ; the billiard-room was deserted. I had an oppor-

tunity this day to introduce Dean Pitferge to Captain
Corsican. My original very much amused the Captain by
telling him the stories whispered about the " Great Eastern."
He attempted to prove to him that it was a bewitched
ship, to which fatal misfortune must happen. The yarn of
the melted engineer greatly pleased the Captain, who,
being a Scotchman, was a lover of the marvellous, but he
could not repress an incredulous smile.

"I see," said Dr. Pitferge, "the Captain has not much
faith in my s'ories."

"Much! that is saying a great deal," replied Corsican.

"Will you believe me, Captain, if I affirm that this ship
is haunted at night?" asked the Doctor, in a serious tone.

"Haunted!" cried the Captain; "what next? Ghosts?
and you believe in them?"

"I believe," replied Pitferge, "I believe what people who
can be depended on have told me. Now, I know some of
the officers on watch, and the sailors also, are quite
unanimous on this point, that during the darkness of
the night a shadow, a vague form, walks the ship. How it
comes there they do not know, neither do they know how
it disappears."

"By St. Dunstan!" exclaimed Captain Corsican, 'we
will watch it well together."

" To-night ? ' asked the Doctor.

"I SEE" SAID DE CITEERGE.

Page 76

" To-night, if you like ; and you, sir," added the Captain, turning to me, " will you keep us company ?"

" No," said I ; " I do not wish to trouble the solitude of this phantom ; besides, I would rather think that our Doctor is joking."

" I am not joking," replied the obstinate Pitferge.

"Come, Doctor," said I. "Do you really believe in the dead coming back to the decks of ships ?"

"I believe in the dead who come to life again," replied the Doctor, and this is the more astonishing as I am a physician."

" A physician !" cried the Captain, drawing back as if the word had made him uneasy.

"Don't be alarmed, Captain," said the Doctor, smiling, good-humouredly ; " I don't practise while travelling."

CHAPTER XV.

THE next day, the 1st of April, the aspect of the sea was
truly spring-like ; it was as green as the meadows beneath
the sun's rays.   This April sunrise on the Atlantic was
superb ; the waves spread themselves out voluptuously,
while porpoises gambolled in the ship's milky track.

When I met Captain Corsican, he informed me that the
ghost announced by the Doctor had not thought proper to
make its appearance.   Undoubtedly, the night was not
dark enough for it.   Then the idea crossed my mind that
it was a joke of Dean Pitferge's, sanctioned by the 1st of
April ; for in America, England, and France this custom is
very popular.   Mystifiers and mystified were not wanting ;
some laughed, others were angry ; I even believe that blows
were exchanged among some of the Saxons, but these
blows never ended in fighting ; for it is well known that in
England duels are liable to very severe punishment ; even
officers and soldiers are not allowed to fight under any
pretext whatever.   The homicide is subject to the most

painful and ignominious punishments. I remember the Doctor telling me the name of an officer who was sent to a convict prison, for ten years, for having mortally wounded his adversary in a very honourable engagement. One can understand, that in face of this severe law duels have entirely disappeared from British customs.

The weather being so fine, a good observation could be made, which resulted in the following statement : Lat. 48°47', and 36° 48' W. L. ; dist., 250 miles only. The slowest of the Transatlantic steamers would have had the right to offer to take us in tow. This state of things very much annoyed Captain Anderson. The engineers attributed the failure of pressure to the insufficient ventilation of the new furnaces ; but for my part, I thought that the diminution of speed was owing to the diameter of the wheels having been imprudently made smaller.

However, to-day, about two o'clock, there was an improvement in the ship's speed ; it was the attitude of the two young lovers which revealed this change to me. Leaning against the bulwarks, they murmured joyful words, clapped their hands, and looked smilingly at the escape-pipes, which were placed near the chimneys, the apertures of which were crowned with a white wreath of vapour. The pressure had risen in the screw boilers ; as yet it was only a feeble breath of air, a wavering blast ; but our young friends drank it in eagerly with their eyes. No, not even Denis Papin could have been more delighted, when he saw the steam half raise the lid of his celebrated saucepan.

"They smoke! they smoke!" cried the young lady, whilst a light breath also escaped from her parted lips.

"Let us go and look at the engine," said the young man, placing her arm in his.

Dean Pitferge had joined me, and we followed the loving couple on to the upper-deck.

"How beautiful is youth!" remarked the Doctor.

"Yes," said I, "youth affianced."

Soon we also were leaning over the railing of the engine-rooms. There, in the deep abyss, at a distance of sixty feet below us, we saw the four long horizontal pistons swaying one towards the other, and with each movement moistened by drops of lubricating oil.

In the meanwhile the young man had taken out his watch, and the girl, leaning over his shoulder, followed the movement of the minute-hand, whilst her lover counted the revolutions of the screw.

"One minute," said she.

" Thirty-seven turns," exclaimed the young man.

"Thirty-seven and a half," observed the Doctor, who had entered into the work.

"And a half," cried the young lady. "You hear, Edward! Thank you, sir," said she, favouring the worthy Pitferge with one of her most pleasing smiles.

CHAPTER XVI.

GOING back to the grand saloon, I saw the following programme posted on the door :—

THIS NIGHT!

PART FIRST

" Ocean Time "	*Mr. Mac Alpine.*
Song : " Beautiful Isle of the Sea "	*Mr. Fwing.*
Reading	*Mr. Afflect.*
Piano solo : " Chant du Berger "	*Mrs. Alloway.*
Scotch Song	*Doctor T——.*

(*Ten minutes interval.*)

PART SECOND.

Piano solo	*Mr. Paul V——.*
Burlesque : " Lady of Lyons "	*Doctor T——.*

G

Entertainment   .   .   .   .   *Sir James Anderson.*
Song: "Happy Moment"   .   .   *Mr. Norville.*
Song: "You Remember"   .   .   *Mr. Ewing.*

FINALE.

"GOD SAVE THE QUEEN."

As may be seen, it was a complete concert, with a first part, entr'acte, second part, and finale ; but it seems there was something wanting in the programme ; for I heard some one mutter behind me, "What! no Mendelssohn."

I turned, and saw that it was a steward, who thus protested against the omission of his favourite music.

I went on deck, and began to look for Mac Elwin. Corsican had just told me that Fabian had left his cabin, and I wanted, without intruding myself on him, to draw him out of his isolation. I found him at the bows ; we talked for some time, but he made no allusion to his past life. At times he was silent and pensive, absorbed in his thoughts, no longer listening to me, and pressing his breast, as if to restrain a painful spasm.

Whilst we were walking together, Harry Drake passed us several times, always the same noisy, gesticulating man, obstructive as would be a windmill in a ball-room. Was I mistaken ? I could not say ; for I had already anticipated it in my mind ; but it seemed to me that Harry

Drake stared at Fabian with a persistency which the latter must have noticed ; for he said to me,—

" Who is that man ? "

" I don't know," I replied.

" I don't like his looks," added Fabian.

Put two ships in the open sea, without wind or tide, and, at last, they will come together. Throw two planets into space, and they will fall one on the other. Place two enemies in the midst of a crowd, and they will inevitably meet ; it is a fatality, a question of time, that is all.

In the evening the concert took place according to the programme ; the grand saloon, filled with the audience, was brilliantly lighted. Through the half-open hatchways might be seen the broad, sunburnt faces, and the great black hands of the sailors ; the doorways were crowded with stewards ; the greater part of the audience—men and women—were seated on side sofas, and in the centre of the saloon, in arm-chairs and lounges, all facing the piano, firmly fastened between the two doors, which opened into the ladies' saloon. From time to time a rolling motion disturbed the audience ; arm-chairs and folding-chairs glided about, a kind of swell caused a similar undulatory movement to all ; they caught hold of one another silently, and without making any joke ; but upon the whole there was not much fear of falling, thanks to the subsidence.

The concert opened with the "Ocean Times." The

"Ocean Times" was a daily newspaper, political, commercial, and literary, which certain passengers had started for the requirements on board. Americans and English took to this sort of pastime; they wrote out their sheet during the day; and let me say, that if the editors were not particular, as to the quality of their articles, their readers were not more so. They were content with little, even with "not enough."

This number for the 1st of April contained a "Great Eastern" leader—tame enough, on general politics—also various facts quite uninteresting to a Frenchman; articles on the money-markets, not particularly comic; curious telegrams, and some rather insipid home news. After all this kind of fun is only amusing to those who make it. The Honourable Mac Alpine, a dogmatical American, read, with earnest gravity, some rather dull lucubrations, which were received by his audience with great applause. He finished his reading with the following news:—

"It is announced that President Johnson has resigned in favour of General Grant."

"It is said that Fernando Cortez is going to attack the Emperor Napoleon the Third, piratically, out of revenge for the latter's conquest of Mexico."

"We are told for a certainty that Pope Pius IX. has designated the Prince Imperial as his successor."

When the "Ocean Times" had been sufficiently

A FINE-LOOKING YOUNG FELLOW.

applauded, the Honourable Mr. Ewing, a fine-looking young fellow, with a tenor voice, warbled "Beautiful Isle of the Sea," with all the harshness of an English throat.

The "reading" appeared to me to have a questionable charm; it was simply two or three pages of a book, read by a worthy Texian, who began in a low voice, and gradually got higher and higher; he also was very much applauded.

The "Shepherd's Song," a piano solo, by Mrs. Alloway, and a Scotch song, sung by Doctor T——, concluded the first part of the programme.

After the ten minutes' interval, during which some of the audience left their seats, the second part of the concert began. The Frenchman, Paul V——, played some charming waltzes, which were noisily encored. One of the ship's doctors on board. a very conceited young man, recited a burlesque scene, a kind of parody on the "Lady of Lyons," a drama very much in vogue in England.

The "burlesque" was succeeded by the "entertainment." What had Sir James Anderson prepared under this name? Was it a conference or a sermon? Neither the one nor the other. Sir James Anderson rose smilingly, drew a pack of cards from his pocket, turned back his white cuffs, and performed some tricks, the simplicity of which was redeemed by the graceful manner in which they were done. Hurrahs and applause.

After the "Happy Moment," and "You Remember,"
sung by Mr. Norville and Mr. Ewing, the programme
announced "God Save the Queen;" but some Americans
begged Paul V——, as he was a Frenchman, to play the
national French Anthem. Immediately my agreeable
countryman began the inevitable "Partant pour la Syrie."
Energetic demands from a party of north-men, who wished
to hear the "Marseillaise," and without being pressed
further, the obedient pianist, with a compliance which be-
tokened rather a musical facility than political convictions,
vigorously attacked the song of Rouget de l'Ile.

This was the grand success of the evening, and the assembly, standing, slowly sang the "National Anthem,"
which prays God to bless the Queen.

Upon the whole this soirée was as good as amateur
soirées generally are; that is to say, it was chiefly a success for the performers and their friends. Fabian did not
show himself there at all.

CHAPTER XVII.

DURING Monday night the sea was very stormy. Once more the partitions began creaking, and again the luggage made its way through the saloons. When I went on deck, about seven o'clock in the morning, the wind had freshened, and it was raining. The officer on watch had ordered the sails to be taken in, so that the steam-ship, left without any support, rolled dreadfully. All this day, the 2nd of April, the deck was deserted, even the saloons were empty, for the passengers had taken refuge in their cabins ; and two-thirds of the guests were missing at lunch and dinner. Whist was impossible, for the tables glided from under the players' hands. The chess-men were unmanage- able. A few of the more fearless stretched themselves on the sofas, reading or sleeping, as many preferred to brave the rain on deck, where the sailors, in their oil-skin jackets and glazed hats, were sedately pacing to and fro. The first officer, well wrapped in his macintosh, and perched on the bridge, was on watch, and in the midst of the hurricane his

small eyes sparkled with delight. This was what the little
man loved, and the steamer rolled to his liking.

The water from the skies and sea mingled in a dense
fog. The atmosphere was grey, and birds flew screech-
ing through the damp mists. At ten o'clock a three-mast
ship was hailed, sailing astern of us, but her nationality
could not be recognized.

At about eleven o'clock the wind abated, and veered to
the north-west. The rain ceased, almost suddenly, blue
sky appeared through the opening in the clouds, the sun
shone out again, and permitted a more or less perfect
observation to be made, which was posted up as follows :—

Lat. 46° 29' N.

Long. 42° 25' W.

Dist., 356 miles.

So that, although the pressure of the boilers had risen, the
ship's speed had not increased ; but this might be attributed to the westerly wind, which caught the ship ahead,
and considerably impeded her progress.

At two o'clock the fog grew dense again, the wind fell
and rose at the same time. The thickness of the fog was
so intense that the officers on the bridge could not see the
men at the bows. These accumulated vapours rising from
the sea constitute the greatest danger of navigation. They
cause accidents which it is impossible to avoid, and a collision at sea is more to be dreaded than a fire.

Thus, in the midst of the fog, officers and sailors were obliged to keep a strict watch, which soon proved to be necessary, for about three o'clock a three-master appeared at less than two hundred yards from the "Great Eastern," her sails disabled by a gust of wind, and no longer answering to her helm. The "Great Eastern" turned in time to avoid her, thanks to the promptitude with which the men on watch warned the steersman. These well-regulated signals are given by means of a bell, fastened to the poop at the bows. One ring signifies ship a-head ; two, ship-starboard ; three, ship a-larboard ; and immediately the man at the helm steers in order to avoid a collision.

The wind did not abate until evening ; however the rolling was nothing to speak of, as the sea was protected by the Newfoundland heights. Another entertainment, by Sir James Anderson, was announced for this day. At the appointed hour the saloon was filled ; but this time it had nothing to do with cards. Sir James Anderson told us the history of the Transatlantic Cable, which he had himself laid. He showed us photographs representing the different engines used for the immersion. He sent round a model of the splice which was used to fasten together the pieces of cable. Finally, very justly merited, the three cheers with which his lecture was received, a great part of which was meant for the Honourable Cyrus Field, promoter of the enterprise, who was present on this occasion.

CHAPTER XVIII.

THE next day, the 3rd of April, from early dawn the horizon wore that peculiar aspect which the English call "blink." It was of that misty white colour which signifies that icebergs are not far distant; in fact the "Great Eastern" was ploughing those seas on which float the first blocks of ice detached from the icebergs in Davis' Straits. A special watch was kept, in order to avoid the rude collision with these enormous blocks.

There was a strong westerly wind blowing; strips of clouds, or rather shreds of vapour, hung over the sea, through which glimpses of blue sky appeared. A dull thudding noise came from the waves tossed by the wind, and drops of water, seemingly pulverized, evaporated in foam.

Neither Fabian, Captain Corsican, nor Doctor Pitferge had yet come on deck, so I went towards the bows, where the junction of the bulwarks formed a comfortable angle, a kind of retreat, in which like a hermit, one could retire

HIS BACK ROUNDED, AND HIS HEAD MUFFLED IN A HOOD.

Page 91.

from the world. I took my place in this corner, sitting on
a skylight, and my feet resting on an enormous pulley;
the wind being dead ahead passed over without touching
me. This was a good place for reflection. From here I
had a view of the whole immensity of the ship; I could
see the long slanting ropes of the rigging at the stern.
On the first level a top-man, hanging in the mizen-
shrouds, held himself up with one hand, whilst with
the other he worked with a remarkable dexterity. On
the deck below him paced the officer on watch, peering
through the mists. On the bridge, at the stern, I caught
a glimpse of an officer, his back rounded, and his head
muffled in a hood, struggling against the gusts of wind.
I could distinguish nothing of the sea, except a bluish
horizontal line discernible behind the paddles. Urged
on by her powerful engines, the narrow stem of the
steam-ship cut the waves, with a hissing sound, like that
when the sides of a boiler are heated by a roaring fire.
But the colossal ship, with the wind a-head, and borne
on three waves, hardly felt the movement of the sea,
which would have shaken any other steamer with its
pitchings.

At half-past twelve the notice stated that we were in
44° 53′ North lat., and 47° 6′ W. long., and had made
two hundred and twenty-seven miles in twenty-four hours
only. The young couple must have scolded the wheels

which did not turn, and the steam which was not at all strong enough to please them.

About three o'clock the sky, swept by the wind, cleared up ; the line of the horizon was once more clearly defined, the wind fell, but for a long while the sea rose in great foam-crested billows. Such a gentle breeze could not cause this swell ; one might have said that the Atlantic was still sulky.

At twenty-five minutes to four a three-mast ship was hailed to larboard. She hoisted her name ; it was the "Illinois," an American ship, on her way to England.

At this moment Lieutenant H—— informed me that we were passing Cape Race point. We were now in the rich coasts where are obtained cod-fish, three of which would suffice to supply England and America if all the roe were hatched. The day passed without any remarkable occurrence ; no accident had as yet thrown Fabian and Harry Drake together, for the Captain and I never lost sight of them. In the evening the same harmless amuse-ment, the same reading, and songs in the grand saloon called forth, as usual, frantic applauses. As an extraordi-nary occurrence a lively discussion broke out between a Northerner and a Texian. The latter demanded an Em-peror for the Southern States. Happily this political dis-cussion, which threatened to degenerate into a quarrel, was put an end to by the timely arrival of an imaginary despatch, addressed to the " Ocean Times," and conceived in these terms : " Captain Semmes, Minister of War, has made the South compensate for its ravages in Alabama."

CHAPTER XIX.

LEAVING the brilliantly lighted saloon I went on deck with Captain Corsican. The night was dark ; not a star in the firmament ; an impenetrable gloom surrounded the ship. The windows of the saloon shone like the mouths of furnaces ; the man on watch, heavily pacing the poop, was scarcely discernible, but one could breathe the fresh air, and the Captain inhaled it with expanded lungs.

"I was stifled in the saloon," said he ; "here at least I can breathe. I require my hundred cubic yards of pure air every twenty-four hours, or I get half suffocated."

"Breathe, Captain, breathe at your ease," said I to him ; "the breeze does not stint your wants. Oxygen is a good thing, but it must be confessed Parisians and Londoners know it only by reputation."

"Yes," replied the Captain, "and they prefer carbonic acid. Ah well ! every one to his liking ; for my own part I detest it, even in champagne."

Thus talking, we paced up and down the deck on the starboard side, sheltered from the wind by the high partitions of the deck cabins. Great wreaths of smoke, illuminated with sparks, curled from the black chimneys ; the noise of the engines accompanied the whistling of the wind in the shrouds, which sounded like the cords of a harp. Mingling with this hubbub, each quarter of an hour, came the cry of the sailors on deck, "All's well, all's well."

In fact no precaution had been neglected to insure the safety of the ship on these coasts frequented by icebergs. The Captain had a bucket of water drawn every half-hour, in order to ascertain the temperature, and if it had fallen one degree he immediately changed his course, for he knew that the " Peruvian " had been seen but a fortnight since blocked up by icebergs in this latitude ; it was therefore a danger to be avoided. His orders for night were to keep a strict look-out. He himself remained on the bridge with an officer each side of him, one at the wheel signal, the other at the screw ; besides these a lieutenant and two men kept watch on the poop, whilst a quarter-master with a sailor stood at the stern ; the passengers might therefore rest quietly.

After noticing these arrangements we went back again to the stern, as we had made up our minds to stay some time longer, walking on deck like peaceful citizens taking an evening stroll in their town squares.

The place seemed deserted. Soon, however, our eyes grew accustomed to the darkness, and we perceived a man leaning perfectly motionless, with his elbow on the railing. Corsican, after looking at him attentively for some time, said to me,—

"It is Fabian."

It was indeed Fabian. We recognized him, but absorbed as he was in a profound contemplation he did not see us. His eyes were fixed on an angle of the upper deck ; I saw them gleam in the dark. What was he looking at ? How could he pierce this black gloom ? I thought it better to leave him to his reflections, but Captain Corsican went up to him.

"Fabian," said he.

Fabian did not answer ; he had not heard. Again Corsican called him. He shuddered, and turned his head for a moment, saying,—

"Hush."

Then with his hand he pointed to a shadow which was slowly moving at the further end of the upper deck. It was this almost invisible figure that Fabian was looking at, and smiling sadly he murmured,—

"The black lady."

I shuddered. Captain Corsican took hold of my arm,

THE BLACK LADY.

Page 96.

and I felt that he also was trembling. The same thought had struck us both. This shadow was the apparition about which Dean Pitferge had spoken.

Fabian had relapsed into his dreamy contemplation. I, with a heaving breast and awe-struck glance, looked at this human figure, the outline of which was hardly discernible ; but presently it became more defined. It came forward, stopped, turned back, and then again advanced, seeming to glide rather than walk. At ten steps from us it stood perfectly still. I was then able to distinguish the figure of a slender female, closely wrapped in a kind of brown burnous, and her face covered with a thick veil.

"A mad woman, a mad woman, is it not ?" murmured Fabian.

It was, indeed, a mad woman ; but Fabian was not asking us : he was speaking to himself.

In the meantime the poor creature came still nearer to us. I thought I could see her eyes sparkle through her veil, when they were fixed on Fabian. She went up to him, Fabian started to his feet, electrified. The veiled woman put her hand on her heart as though counting its pulsation, then, gliding swiftly away, she disappeared behind the angle of the upper deck. Fabian staggered, and fell on his knees, his hands stretched out before him.

" It is she," he murmured.

Then shaking his head.—

" What an hallucination ! " he added.

Captain Corsican then took him by the hand.

" Come, Fabian, come," said he, and he led away his unhappy friend.

CHAPTER XX.

CORSICAN and I could no longer doubt but that it was Ellen, Fabian's betrothed, and Harry Drake's wife. Chance had brought all three together on the same ship. Fabian had not recognized her, although he had cried, "It is she, it is she!" and how was it possible that he could have done so? But he was not mistaken in saying, "A mad woman!" Ellen was mad, undoubtedly ; grief, despair, love frozen in her heart, contact with the worthless man who had snatched her from Fabian, ruin, misery, and shame had broken her spirit. It was on this subject that Corsican and I spoke the following morning. We had no doubt as to the identity of the young woman ; it was Ellen, whom Harry Drake was dragging with him to the American continent. The Captain's eyes glowed with a dark fire at the thought of this wretch, and I felt my heart stir within me. What were we against the husband, the master? Nothing. But now, what was most important, was to prevent another meeting between Fabian and Ellen, for Fabian could not fail at last to recognize his betrothed, and thus the catastrophe we wished to avoid would be brought about.

At the same time we had reason to hope that these two poor creatures would not see each other again, as the unhappy Ellen never appeared in the daytime, either in the saloons or on the deck. Only at night, perhaps eluding her gaoler, she came out to bathe herself in the damp air, and demand of the wind a smooth passage. In four days, at the latest, the "Great Eastern" must reach New York harbour ; therefore we might hope that accident would not dally with our watchfulness, and that Fabian would not discover Ellen during this time ; but we made our calculations without thinking of events.

The steamer's course had been slightly altered in the night, three times the ship, being in water twenty-seven degrees Fahrenheit—that is to say, five degrees below zero, had been turned towards the south. There was no longer any doubt of icebergs being very near, for the sky that morning had a peculiarly brilliant aspect ; the atmosphere was misty, and the northern sky glittered with an intense reverberation, evidently produced by the powerful reflection from the icebergs. There was a piercing wind, and about ten o'clock the deck was powdered by a slight snow fall ; then dense fog surrounded us, in which we gave warning of our approach, by deafening whistles, which scared away the flocks of sea-gulls in the ship's yards. At half-past ten, the fog having cleared off, a screw steamer appeared on the horizon, a-starboard, the white tops of her chimneys indicating that she was an emigrant ship, belonging to the Inman Company.

Before lunch several of the passengers organized a pool, which could not fail to please those fond of betting and gambling. The result of this pool was not to be known for four days ; it was what is called the "pilot's pool." When a ship arrives at the land-falls every one knows that a pilot comes on board ; so they divide the twenty-four hours of the day and night into forty-eight half-hours, or ninety-six quarters, according to the number of the passengers. Each player stakes one dollar, and draws one of the half or quarter hours : the winner of the forty-eight or ninety-six dollars is the one during whose quarter of an hour the pilot comes on board. From this it may be seen that the game is very simple ; it is not a race-course, but a quarter-of-an-hour race.

It was a Canadian, the Honourable MacAlpine, who undertook the management of the affair. He easily collected ninety-six players, including several professed gamblers, not the least among those ready for gain. I, following the general example, staked my dollar, and fate allotted me the ninety-fourth quarter ; it was a bad

number, and one which left me no chance of profit. The
fact is, these divisions are reckoned from noon to noon, so
that there are night as well as day quarters; and as it is
very seldom that ships venture close in in the dark, the
chance of a pilot coming on board then is very small.
However, I easily consoled myself. Going down into the
saloon, I saw a lecture announced. The Utah missionary
was going to hold a meeting on Mormonism; a good
opportunity for those wishing to initiate themselves in the
mysteries of the City of Saints; besides, this Elder, Mr.
Hatch, was an orator of no mean power. The execution
could not fail to be worthy of the work. The announce-
ment of the conference was received very favourably by
the passengers.

The observation posted up was as follows :—

Lat. 42° 32′ N.

Long. 51° 59′ W.

Course, 254 miles.

About three o'clock in the afternoon the steersman sig-
naled a large four-mast steamer, which slightly changed its
course, in order to give the "Great Eastern" its number.
It was the "Atlanta," one of the largest boats running
between London and New York, calling at Brest on the
way. After having saluted us, which we returned, in a
short time she was out of sight.

At this moment Dean Pitferge, in a vexed tone,

informed me that Mr. Hatch's lecture was forbidden, as the wives of the puritans on board did not approve or their husbands becoming acquainted with the mysteries of Mormonism.

CHAPTER XXI.

AT four o'clock, the sky, which had been overcast, cleared up, the sea grew calm, and the ship was so steady, one might almost have thought oneself on *terra firma*—this gave the passengers the idea of getting up races. Epsom turf could not have afforded a better coursing-ground, and as for horses, they were well replaced by pure Scotchmen, as good as any "Gladiator," or "La Touque." The news soon spread, sportsmen immediately hurried to the field. An Englishman, the Hon. J. Mac Carthy, was appointed commissioner, and the competitors presented themselves without delay. They were half a dozen sailors, kind of centaurs, man and horse at the same time, all ready to try for the prize.

The two boulevards formed the race-course, the runners were to go three times round the ship, thus making a course of about 1300 yards, which was quite enough. Soon the galleries were invaded by crowds of spectators,

all armed with opera-glasses. Some of them had hoisted
the "green sail," no doubt to shelter themselves from
the spray of the Atlantic. Carriages were missing, I
must confess, but not the rank, where they might
have ranged in file. Ladies in gay costumes were hur-
rying on to the upper-decks; the scene was charming.

Fabian, Captain Corsican, Dr. Pitferge and I had taken
our places on the poop, which was what might be
called the centre of action. Here the real gentlemen
riders were assembled ; in front of us was the starting and
winning post. Betting soon began with a true British
animation. Considerable sums of money were staked, but
only from the appearance of the racers, whose qualifications
had not as yet been inscribed in the "stud-book." It was
not without uneasiness that I saw Harry Drake interfering
in the preparations with his usual audacity, discussing, dis-
puting, and settling affairs in a tone which admitted of no
reply. Happily, although Fabian had risked some pounds
in the race, he appeared quite indifferent to the noise ; he
kept himself aloof from the others, and it was quite evident
his thoughts were far off.

Among the racers who offered themselves, two particularly attracted the public attention. Wilmore, a small,
thin, wiry Scotchman, with a broad chest and sharp eyes,
was one of the favourites ; the other, an Irishman named
O'Kelly, a tall, supple fellow, balanced the chance with

Wilmore, in the eyes of connoisseurs. Three to one was
asked on him, and for myself partaking the general infa-
tuation. I was going to risk a few dollars on him, when
the Doctor said to me,—

"Choose the little one; believe me, the tall one is
no go."

"What do you say?"

"I say," replied the Doctor, "that the tall one is not
genuine; he may have a certain amount of speed, but he
has no bottom.   The little one, on the contrary, is of
pure Scotch race; look how straight his body is on his
legs, and how broad and pliant his chest is; he is a man
who will lead more than once in the race.   Bet on him,
I tell you; you won't regret it."

I took the learned doctor's advice, and bet on Wilmore; as to the other four, they were not even dis-
cussed.

They drew for places; chance favoured the Irishman,
who had the rope-side; the six runners were placed along
the line, bounded by the posts, so that there was no unfair
start to be feared.

The commissioner gave the signal, and the departure
was hailed by a loud hurrah.   It was soon evident that
Wilmore and O'Kelly were professional runners; without
taking any notice of their rivals, who passed them breathless, they ran with their bodies thrown slightly forward,

heads very erect, arms tightly pressed against their chests, and holding their fists firmly in front.

In the second round O'Kelly and Wilmore were in a line, having distanced their exhausted competitors. They obviously verified the Doctor's saying,—

" It is not with the legs, but with the chest that one runs; ham-strings are good, but lungs are better."

At the last turning but one the spectators again cheered their favourites. Cries and hurrahs broke out on all sides.

" The little one will win," said Pitferge to me. " Look, he is not even panting, and his rival is breathless."

Wilmore indeed looked calm and pale, whilst O'Kelly was steaming like a damp hay-stack ; he was " pumped out," to use a sportsman's slang expression, but both of them kept the same line. At last they passed the upper decks ; the hatchway of the engine-rooms, the winning-post.

" Hurrah ! hurrah ! for Wilmore," cried some.

" Hurrah ! for O'Kelly," chimed in others.

" Wilmore has won."

" No, they are together."

The truth was Wilmore had won, but by hardly half a head so the Honourable Mac Carthy decided. However, the discussion continued, and even came to words The partisans of the Irishman, and particularly Harry Drake, maintained that it was a " dead heat," and that they ought to go again.

But at this moment, urged by an irresistible impulse, Fabian went up to Harry Drake, and said to him in a cold tone,—

"You are wrong, sir, the winner was the Scotch sailor."

"What do you say?" he asked, in a threatening tone.

"I say you are wrong," answered Fabian quietly.

"Undoubtedly," retorted Drake, "because you bet on Wilmore."

"I was for O'Kelly, like yourself; I lost, and I have paid."

"Sir," cried Drake, "do you pretend to teach me?—"

But he did not finish his sentence, for Captain Corsican had interposed between him and Fabian, with the intention of taking up the quarrel. He treated Drake with supreme contempt, but evidently Drake would not pick a quarrel with him; so when Corsican had finished, he crossed his arms, and addressing himself to Fabian,—

"This gentleman," said he, with an evil smile, "this gentleman wants some one to fight his battles for him."

Fabian grew pale, he would have sprung at Drake, but I held him back, and the scoundrel's companions dragged him away; not, however, before he had cast a look of hatred at his enemy.

Captain Corsican and I went below with Fabian, who contented himself by saying, "The first opportunity I have, I will box that impudent fellow's ears."

HE TREATED DRAKE WITH SUPREME CONTEMPT.

Page 108

CHAPTER XXII.

FROM Thursday night to Saturday the "Great Eastern" was crossing the Gulf Stream, the water of which is of a dark colour, the surface of the current forcing its way against the waters of the Atlantic, is even slightly convex. It is, in fact, a river running between two liquid shores, and one of the largest in the world, for it reduces the Amazon and Mississippi to mere brooks in comparison.

This day, the 5th of April, began with a magnificent sunrise, the waves glittered, and a warm south-west wind was wafted through the rigging. It was the beginning of the fine weather ; the sun, which had clothed the fields of the continent with verdure, caused fresh costumes to bloom on board. Vegetation is sometimes behind-hand, but fashion never. Soon the Boulevards, filled with groups of promenaders, looked like the Champs Elysées on a fine Sunday afternoon in May.

I did not see Captain Corsican once that morning ;

wishing to hear of Fabian, I went to his cabin, and knocked at the door, but getting no answer I opened it and went in. Fabian was not there. I went on deck again, but could find neither my friends nor the Doctor; the idea then crossed my mind to find out where the unfortunate Ellen was confined. What cabin did she occupy? Where had Drake shut her up? In whose care was the poor creature left, when Drake abandoned her for whole days? Most likely with some disinterested stewardess, or an indifferent nurse. I wished to know how it was, not from any vain motive of curiosity, but simply in Ellen and Fabian's interest, if it was only to prevent a meeting, always to be dreaded.

I began my search with the cabin near the ladies' saloon, and went along the passages of both stories. This inspection was easy enough, as the names of the occupants were written on each door, in order to facilitate the steward's work. I did not see Harry Drake's name, but this did not surprise me much, as I had no doubt he had preferred the more isolated cabins at the stern. In matter of comfort, however, no difference existed between the cabins at the bows and those at the stern, for the *Freighters* had only admitted one class of passengers.

I next went towards the dining saloons, keeping carefully to the side passages which wound between the double row of cabins. All these rooms were occupied, and all had the name of the passengers outside, but Harry Drake's name was not to be seen. This time the absence of his name astonished me, for I thought I had been all over our Floating City, and I was not aware of any part more secluded than this.

I inquired of a steward, who told me there were yet a hundred cabins behind the dining saloons.

" How do you get to them ?" I asked.

" By a staircase at the end of the upper deck."

" Thank you, and can you tell me which cabin Mr. Harry Drake occupies ?"

" I do not know, sir," replied the steward.

Again I went on deck, and following the steward's direction at last came to the door at the top of the stairs. This staircase did not lead to any large saloons, but simply to a dimly-lighted landing, round which was arranged a double row of cabins. Harry Drake could hardly have found a more favourable place in which to hide Ellen.

The greater part of the cabins were unoccupied. I went along the landing, a few names were written on the doors, but only two or three at the most. Harry Drake's name was not among them, and as I had made a very minute inspection of this compartment, I was very much disappointed at my ill success. I was going away when suddenly a vague, almost inaudible murmur caught my ear, it proceeded from the left side of the passage. I went towards the place ; the sounds, at first faint, grew louder, and I distinguished a kind of plaintive song, or rather melopœia, the words of which did not reach me.

I listened ; it was a woman singing, but in this uncon-scious voice one could recognize a mournful wail. Might not this voice belong to the mad woman? My presenti-ments could not deceive me. I went quietly nearer to the cabin, which was numbered 775. It was the last in this dim passage, and must have been lighted by the lowest light-ports in the hull of the " Great Eastern ;" there was no name on the door, and Harry Drake had no desire that any one should know the place where he confined Ellen.

I could not distinctly hear the voice of the unfortunate woman ; her song was only a string of unconnected sentences like one speaking in sleep, but at the same time it was sweet and plaintive.

Although I had no means of recognizing her identity, I had no doubt but that it was Ellen singing.

I listened for some minutes, and was just going away, when I heard a step on the landing. Could it be Harry Drake ? I did not wish him to find me here, for Fabian and Ellen's sake; fortunately I could get on deck, with-out being seen, by a passage leading round the cabins. However, I stopped to know who it really was that I had heard. The darkness partially hid me, and standing

FABIAN WENT NEAR TO THE CABIN DOORS.

Page 113.

behind an angle of the passage I could see without being myself in sight.

In the meantime the sound of the footsteps had ceased, and with it, as a strange coincident, Ellen's voice. I waited and soon the song began again, and the boards creaked under a stealthy tread ; I leaned forward and, in the dim, uncertain light which glimmered through the creaks of the cabin doors, I recognized Fabian.

It was my unhappy friend! What instinct could have led him to this place? Had he then discovered the young woman's retreat before me? I did not know what to think. Fabian slowly advanced along the passage, listening, following the voice, as if it was a thread drawing him unconsciously on, and in spite of himself. It seemed to me that the song grew fainter as he approached, and that the thread thus held was about to break. Fabian went quite near to the cabin doors and then stopped.

How those sad accents must have rent his heart! and how his whole being must have thrilled as he caught some tone in the voice, which reminded him of the past! But how was it, ignorant as he was of Harry Drake being on board, that he had any suspicion of Ellen's presence? No, it was impossible; he had only been attracted by the plaintive accents which insensibly responded to the great grief weighing down his spirit.

Fabian was still listening. What was he going to do?

I

Would he call to the mad woman? And what if Ellen suddenly appeared? Everything was dangerous in this situation! However, Fabian came nearer still to the door of her cabin; the song, which was growing fainter and fainter, suddenly died away, and a piercing shriek was heard.

Had Ellen, by a magnetic communication, felt him whom she loved so near her? Fabian's attitude was desperate: he had gathered himself up. Was he going to break the door open? I thought he would, so I rushed up to him.

He recognized me; I dragged him away, and he made no resistance, but asked me in a hollow voice, "Do you know who that unhappy woman is?"

" No, Fabian, no."

" It is the mad woman," said he, in an unnatural voice, "but this madness is not without remedy. I feel that a little devotion, a little love, would cure the poor woman."

" Come, Fabian," said I, "come away."

We went on deck, but Fabian did not utter another word. I did not leave him, however, until he had reached nis cabin.

CHAPTER XXIII.

SOME moments later 1 met Captain Corsican, and told him of the scene I had just witnessed. He understood, as well as I did, that the situation of affairs was growing more and more serious. Ah! could I have foreseen all that would happen, how I should have longed to hasten the speed of the "Great Eastern," and put the broad ocean between Fabian and Harry Drake!

On leaving each other, Captain Corsican and I agreed to watch the actors in this drama more narrowly than ever.

The "Australasian," a Cunard steamer, running between Liverpool and New York, was expected this day. She was to leave America on Wednesday morning, and therefore would not be long before passing us. A watch was kept; however, she did not come in sight.

About eleven o'clock the English passengers organized a subscription on behalf of the wounded on board, some of whom had not been able to leave the hospital ; among them was the boatswain, threatened with an incurable lameness. There was soon a long list of signatures, not however, without some objections having been raised.

At noon a very exact observation was able to be made—

Long. 58°, 37' W.

Lat. 41° 41' 11" N.

Course, 257 miles.

We had the latitude to a second. When the young engaged couple read the notice they did not look remarkably pleased, and they had good reason to be discontented with the steam.

Before lunch, Captain Anderson wishing to divert the passengers from the tedium of their long voyage, arranged some gymnastic exercises, which he directed in person. About fifty unemployed men, each armed, like himself, with a stick, imitated all his movements with a strict exactitude. These improvised gymnasts, with their firm set mouths, worked as methodically as a band of riflemen on parade.

Another entertainment was announced for this evening. I was not present, for the same amusement, night after night, only wearied me. A new paper, a rival of the " Ocean Times," was to be the great attraction.

I passed the first hours of the night on deck ; the sea heaved, and gave warning of stormy weather, and although the sky was perfectly serene, the rolling grew more empha-

sized. Lying on a seat of the upper deck, I could admire
the host of constellations with which the firmament was
bespangled, and although there are only 5000 stars, in
the whole extent of the celestial sphere, which are visible to
the naked eye, this evening I thought I could see millions.
There, along the horizon, trailed the tail of Pegasus, in all
its zodiacal magnificence, like the starry robe of the queen
of fairies. The Peliades ascended the celestial heights
with Gemini, who, in spite of their name, do not rise one
after the other, like the heroes of the fable. Taurus looked
down on me with his great fiery eye, whilst Vega, our
future polar-star, shone brilliantly, high up in the azure
vault, and not far from her was the circle of diamonds,
which form the constellation of Corona Borealis. All
these stationary constellations seemed to move with the
pitching of the vessel, and in one lurch I saw the main-
mast describe a distinct arc of a circle from β, in the
Great Bear, to Altair in the Eagle, whilst the moon,
already low in the heavens, dipped her crescent in the
horizon.

CHAPTER XXIV.

THE night was stormy, the steam-ship, beaten by the waves, rolled frightfully, without being disabled ; the furniture was knocked about with loud crashes, and the crockery began its clatter again. The wind had evidently freshened, and besides this the " Great Eastern " was now in those coasts where the sea is always rough.

At six o'clock in the morning I dragged myself to the staircase, leading on to the upper decks. By clutching at the balusters, and taking advantage of a lurch or two, I succeeded in climbing the steps, and with some difficulty managed to reach the poop. The place was deserted, if one may so qualify a place where was Dr. Pitferge. The worthy man, with his back rounded as a protection against the wind, was leaning against the railing, with his right leg wound tightly round one of the rails. He beckoned for me to go to him—with his head, of course, for he could not spare his hands, which held him up against

the violence of the tempest. After several queer movements, twisting myself like an analide, I reached the upper-
deck, where I buttressed myself, after the doctor's fashion.
"We are in for it!" cried he to me; "this will last.
Heigh ho! this 'Great Eastern!' Just at the moment of
arrival, a cyclone, a veritable cyclone is commanded on
purpose for her."

The Doctor spoke in broken sentences, for the wind cut
short his words, but I understood him; the word cyclone
carried its explanation with it.

It is well known that these whirlwinds, called hurricanes
in the Indian and Atlantic Oceans, tornadoes on the coast
of Africa, simoons in the desert, and typhoons in the
Chinese Sea, are tempests of such formidable power, that
they imperil the largest ships.

Now the "Great Eastern" was caught in a cyclone
How would this giant make head against it?

"Harm will come to her," repeated Dean Pitferge.
"Look, how she dives into the billows."

This was, indeed, the exact position of the steam-ship,
whose stern disappeared beneath the mountains of waves,
which swept violently against her. It was not possible to
see to any distance: there were all the symptoms of a
storm, which broke forth in its fury about seven o'clock. The
ocean heaved terrifically, the small undulations between
the large waves entirely disappeared under an overwhelm-

ing wind, the foam-crested billows clashed together, in the wildest uproar, every moment; the waves grew higher, and the "Great Eastern," cutting through them, pitched frightfully.

"There are but two courses now to choose from," said the Doctor, with the self-possession of a seaman, "either to put the ship's head on to the waves, working with a minimum speed, or take flight and give up the struggle with this baffling sea; but Captain Anderson will do neither one thing nor the other."

"And why not?" I asked.

"Because—" replied the doctor, "because something must happen."

Turning round, I saw the Captain, the first officer, and the chief engineer, muffled in their macintoshes, and clutching at the railings of the bridge; they were enveloped in spray from head to foot. The Captain was smiling as usual, the first officer laughed, and showed his white teeth, at the sight of the ship pitching enough to make one think the masts and chimneys were coming down.

Nevertheless I was really astonished at the Captain's obstinacy. At half-past seven, the aspect of the Atlantic was terrible; the sea swept right across the deck at the bows. I watched this grand sight; this struggle between the giant and the billows, and to a certain extent I could sympathize with the Captain's wilfulness; but I was forgetting that the power of the sea is infinite, and that nothing made by the hand of man can resist it ; and, indeed, powerful as she was, our ship was at last obliged to fly before the tempest.

Suddenly, at about eight o'clock, a violent shock was felt, caused by a formidable swoop of the sea, which struck the ship on her fore larboard quarter.

" That was not a box on the ear, it was a blow in the face," said the Doctor to me.

And the blow had evidently bruised us, for spars appeared on the crests of the waves. Was it part of our ship that was making off in this manner, or the *débris* of a wreck ?

On a sign from the Captain, the "Great Eastern" shifted her course, in order to avoid the spars, which threatened to get entangled in the paddles. Looking more attentively, I saw that the sea had carried off the bulwarks on the larboard side, which were fifty feet above the surface of the water ; the jambs were broken, the taggers torn away, and the shattered remnants of glass still trembled in their casements. The "Great Eastern" had staggered beneath the shock, but she continued her way with an indomitable audacity. It was necessary, as quickly as possible, to remove the spars which encumbered the ship at the bows, and in order to do this it was indispensable to avoid the sea, but the steam-ship obstinately continued to make head against the waves. The spirit of her captain seemed to animate her; he did not want to yield, and yield he would not. An officer and some men were sent to the bows to clear the deck.

" Mind," said the Doctor to me, "the moment of the catastrophe is not far off."

The sailors went towards the bows, whilst we fastened ourselves to the second mast, and looked through the spray, which fell in showers over us with each wave. Suddenly there was another swoop more violent than the first, and the sea poured through the barricading by the opened breach, tore off an enormous sheet of cast-iron which covered the bit of the bows, broke away the massive top of the hatchway leading to the crew's berths, and lashing against the starboard barricadings, swept them off like the sheets of a sail.

The men were knocked down; one of them, an officer, half-drowned, shook his red whiskers, and picked himself up; then seeing one of the sailors lying unconscious across an anchor, he hurried towards him, lifted him on his shoulders and carried him away. At this moment the rest of the crew escaped through the broken hatchway. There were three feet of water in the tween-decks, new spars covered the sea, and amongst other things several thousand of the dolls, which my countryman had thought to acclimatize in America; these little bodies, torn from

ONE OF THE SAILORS LYING UNCONSCIOUS.

Page 163

their cases by the sea, danced on the summits of the waves, and under less serious circumstances the sight would have been truly ludicrous. In the meantime the inundation was gaining on us, large bodies of water were pouring in through the opened gaps, and according to the engineer, the "Great Eastern" shipped more than two thousand tons of water, enough to float a frigate of the largest size.

"Well!" exclaimed the Doctor, whose hat had been blown off in the hurricane, "to keep in this position is impossible ; it is fool-hardy to hold on any longer : we ought to take flight, the steam-ship going with her battered stem ahead, is like a man swimming between two currents, with his mouth open."

This Captain Anderson understood at last, for I saw him run to the little wheel on the bridge which commanded the movement of the rudder, the steam immediately rushed into the cylinders at the stern, and the giant turning like a canoe made head towards the north, and fled before the storm.

At this moment, the Captain, generally so calm and self-possessed, cried angrily,—

"My ship is disgraced."

CHAPTER XXV.

SCARCELY had the " Great Eastern " tacked and presented
her stern to the waves, than the pitching gave way to
perfect steadiness ; breakfast was served, and the greater
part of the passengers, reassured by the ship's stillness,
came into the dining-rooms, and took their repast without
fear of another shock. Not a plate fell off the table, and
not a glass emptied its contents on to the cloth, although
the racks had not even been put up. But three quarters of
an hour later the furniture was set in motion again, and
the crockery clattered together on the pantry shelves, for
the " Great Eastern " had resumed her westerly course,
which for the time had been interrupted.

I went on deck again with Dr. Pitferge, who seeing tne
man belonging to the dolls said to him,—

" Your little people have been put to a severe test,
sir ; those poor babies will never prattle in the United
States."

"Pshaw!" replied the enterprising Parisian, "the stock was insured, and my secret has not perished with it."

It was evident my countryman was not a man to be easily disheartened, he bowed to us with a pleasant smile, and we continued our way to the stern, where a steersman told us that the rudder-chains had been jammed in the interval between the two swoops.

"If that accident had happened when we were turning," said Pitferge to me, "I cannot say what would have become of us, for the sea would have rushed in, in overwhelming torrents; the steam pumps have already begun to reduce the water, but there is more coming yet."

"And what of the unfortunate sailor?" asked I of the Doctor.

"He is severely wounded on his head, poor fellow! he is a young married fisherman, the father of two children, and this is his first voyage. The Doctor seems to think there is hope of his recovery, and that is what makes me fear for him, but we shall soon see for ourselves. A report was spread that several men had been washed overboard, but happily there was no foundation for it."

"We have resumed our course at last," said I.

"Yes," replied the Doctor, "the westerly course, against wind and tide, there is no doubt about that," added he, catching hold of a kevel to prevent himself from rolling on the deck. "Do you know what I should do with the 'Great Eastern' if she belonged to me? No. Well, I would make a pleasure-boat of her, and charge 10,000 francs ahead; there would only be millionnaires on board, and people who were not pressed for time. I would take a month or six weeks going from England to America; the ship never against the waves, and the wind always ahead or astern; there should be no rolling, no pitching, and I would pay a 100*l.* in any case of sea-sickness."

"That is a practical idea," said I.

"Yes," replied Pitferge, "there's money to be gained or lost by that!"

In the meantime the "Great Eastern" was slowly but steadily continuing her way; the swell was frightful, but her straight stem cut tne waves regularly, and shipped no more water. It was no longer a metal mountain making against a mountain of water, but as sedentary as a rock the "Great Eastern" received the billows with perfect indifference. The rain fell in torrents, and we were obliged to take refuge under the eaves of the grand saloon; with the shower the violence of the wind and sea assuaged; the western sky grew clear, and the last black clouds vanished in the opposite horizon; at ten o'clock the hurricane sent us a farewell gust.

At noon an observation was able to be made and was as follows :—

Lat. 49° 50', N.

Long. 61° 57', W.

Course, 193 miles.

This considerable diminution in the ship's speed could only be attributed to the tempest, which during the night and morning had incessantly beaten against the ship, and a tempest so terrible that one of the passengers, almost an inhabitant of the Atlantic, which he had crossed forty-four times, declared he had never seen the like. The engineer even said that during the storm, when the "Great Eastern" was three days in the trough of the sea, the ship had never been attacked with such violence, and it must be repeated that even if this admirable steam-ship did go at an inferior speed, and rolled decidedly too much, she nevertheless presented a sure security against the fury of the sea, which she resisted like a block, owing to the perfect homogenity of her construction.

But let me also say, however powerful she might be, it was not right to expose her, without any reason whatever, to a baffling sea; for however strong, however imposing a ship may appear, it is not "disgraced" because it flies before the tempest. A commander ought always to remember that a man's life is worth more than the mere satisfaction of his own pride. In any case, to be obstinate is blameable, and to be wilful is dangerous. A recent incident in which a dreadful catastrophe happened to a

Transatlantic steamer shows us that a captain ought not to struggle blindly against the sea, even when he sees the boat of a rival company creeping ahead.

CHAPTER XXVI.

IN the meantime the pumps were exhausting the lake which had been formed in the hold of the "Great Eastern," like a lagoon in the middle of an island; powerfully and rapidly worked by steam they speedily restored to the Atlantic that which belonged to it. The rain had ceased and the wind freshened again, but the sky, swept by the tempest, was clear. I stayed several hours after dark walking on deck. Great floods of light poured from the half-opened hatchways of the saloons, and at the stern stretched a phosphorescent light as far as the eye could reach, streaked here and there by the luminous crests of the waves. The stars reflected in the lactescent water appeared and disappeared, as though peering through rapidly driving clouds. Night had spread her sombre covering far and near; forward roared the thunder of the wheels, whilst beneath me I heard the clanking of the rudder-chains.

Going back to the saloon door I was surprised to see

K

there a compact crowd of spectators, and to hear vociferous
applauses, for, in spite of the day's disasters, the entertainment was taking place as usual. Not a thought of the
wounded and, perhaps, dying sailor. The assembly seemed
highly animated, and loud hurrahs hailed the appearance of
a troop of minstrels on board the "Great Eastern." The
niggers—black, or blackened, according to their origin—were
no others than sailors in disguise. They were dressed in
cast-off trumpery, ornamented with sea-biscuits for buttons;
the opera-glasses which they sported were composed of two
bottles fastened together, and their jew's-harps consisted
of catgut stretched on cork. These merry-andrews were
amusing enough upon the whole; they sang comic songs,
and improvised a mixture of puns and cock-and-bull
stories. The uproarious cheers with which their perform-
ances were greeted only made them increase their con-
tortions and grimaces, until one of them, as nimble as a
monkey, finished the performance by dancing the sailor's
hornpipe.

However amusing the minstrels may have been, they had
not succeeded in attracting all the passengers. Numbers of
them had flocked to their usual haunt, the "smoking-room,"
and were eagerly pressing round the gaming-tables, where
enormous stakes were being made, some defending their
acquisitions during the voyage, others trying to conquer
fate by making rash wagers at the last moment. The room

A TROOP OF MINSTRELS.

was in a violent uproar, one could hear the voice of the
money agent crying the stakes, the oaths of the losers, the
clinking of gold, and the rustling of dollar-papers ; then
there was a sudden lull, the uproar was silenced by a bold
stake, but as soon as the result was known the noise was
redoubled.

I very seldom entered the smoking-room, for I have a
horror of gambling. It is always a vulgar and often an
unhealthy pastime, and it is a vice which does not go alone ;
the man who gambles will find himself capable of any evil.
Here reigned Harry Drake in the midst of his parasites,
here also flourished those adventurers who were going to
seek their fortunes in America. I always avoided a meeting
with these boisterous men, so this evening I passed the
door without going in, when my attention was arrested by
a violent outburst of cries and curses. I listened, and, after
a moment's silence, to my great astonishment I thought I
could distinguish Fabian's voice. What could he be doing
in this place ? Had he come here to look for his enemy,
and thus the catastrophe, until now avoided, been brought
about ?

I quickly pushed the door open: at this moment the
uproar was at its height. In the midst of the crowd of
gamblers I saw Fabian standing facing Harry Drake. I
hurried towards him, Harry Drake had undoubtedly grossly
insulted him, for Fabian was aiming a blow with his fist at

him, and if it did not reach the place it was intended for, it was only because Corsican suddenly appeared and stopped him with a quick gesture.

But, addressing himself to his enemy, Fabian said, in a cold, sarcastic tone,—

"Do you accept that blow?"

"Yes," replied Drake, "and here is my card!"

Thus, in spite of our efforts, an inevitable fatality had brought these two deadly enemies together. It was too late to separate them now, events must take their course. Captain Corsican looked at me, and I was surprised to see sadness rather than annoyance in his eyes.

In the meantime Fabian picked up the card which Harry Drake had thrown on the table. He held it between the tips of his fingers as if loath to touch it. Corsican was pale, and my heart beat wildly. At last Fabian looked at the card, and read the name on it, then with a voice stifled by passion he cried,—

"Harry Drake! you! you! you!"

"The same, Captain Mac Elwin," quietly replied Fabian's rival.

We were not deceived, if Fabian was ignorant until now of Drake's name, the latter was only too well aware of Fabian's presence on the "Great Eastern."

"DO YOU ACCEPT THAT BLOW?"

Page 132.

CHAPTER XXVII.

THE next day, at break of dawn, I went in search of Captain Corsican, whom I found in the grand saloon. He had passed the night with Fabian, who was still suffering from the shock which the name of Ellen's husband had given him. Did a secret intuition tell him that Drake was not alone on board? Had Ellen's presence been revealed to him by the appearance of this man? Lastly, could he guess that the poor crazed woman was the young girl whom he so fondly loved? Corsican could not say, for Fabian had not uttered one word all night.

Corsican resented Fabian's wrongs with a kind of brotherly feeling. The intrepid nature of the latter had from childhood irresistibly attracted him, and he was now in the greatest despair.

"I came in too late," said he to me. "Before Fabian could have raised his hand, I ought to have struck that wretch."

"Useless violence," replied I. "Harry Drake would not

have risked a quarrel with you; he has a grudge against Fabian, and a meeting between the two had become inevitable."

"You are right," said the Captain. "That rascal has got what he wanted; he knew Fabian, his past life, and his love. Perhaps Ellen, deprived of reason, betrayed her secret thoughts, or, rather, did not Drake before his marriage learn from the loyal young woman all he was ignorant of regarding her past life? Urged by a base impulse, and finding himself in contact with Fabian, he has waited for an opportunity in which he could assume the part of the offended. This scoundrel ought to be a clever duellist."

"Yes," replied I. "He has already had three or four encounters of the kind."

"My dear sir," said the Captain, "it is not the duel in itself which I fear for Fabian. Captain McElwin is one of those who never trouble themselves about danger, but it is the result of this engagement which is to be dreaded. If Fabian were to kill this man, however vile he may be, it would place an impossible barrier between Ellen and himself, and Heaven knows, the unhappy woman needs a support, like Fabian, in the state she now is."

"True," said I; "whatever happens we can but hope that Harry Drake will fall. Justice is on our side."

"Certainly," replied the Captain, "but one cannot help

feeling distressed to think that even at the risk of my own life I could not have spared Fabian this."

"Captain," said I, taking the hand of this devoted friend, "Drake has not sent his seconds yet, so that, although circumstances are against us, I do not despair."

" Do you know any means of preventing the duel ?"

" None at present; at the same time, if the meeting must take place, it seems to me that it can only do so in America, and before we get there, chance, which has brought about this state of things, will, perhaps, turn the scales in our favour."

Captain Corsican shook his head like a man who had no faith in the efficacy of chance in human affairs. At this moment Fabian went up the stairs leading to the deck. I only saw him for a moment, but I was struck by the deadly pallor of his face. The wound had been reopened, and it was sad to see him wandering aimlessly about, trying to avoid us.

Even friendship may be troublesome at times, and Corsican and I thought it better to respect his grief rather than interfere with him. But suddenly Fabian turned, and coming towards us, said,—

" The mad woman, was she ! It was Ellen, was it not ? Poor Ellen ! "

He was still doubtful, and went away without waiting for an answer, which we had not the courage to give.

CHAPTER XXVIII.

AT noon, Drake had not sent Fabian his seconds to my knowledge, and these were preliminaries which could not be dispensed with, if Drake determined to demand immediate satisfaction. Might we not take hope from this delay? I knew that the Saxon race do not regard a debt of honour as we do, and that duels had almost disappeared from English customs, for, as I have already said, not only is there a severe law against duellists, but, moreover, the public opinion is strongly averse to them. At the same time, in this, which was an uncommon case, the engagement had evidently been voluntarily sought for; the offended had, so to speak, provoked the offender, and my reasonings always tended to the same conclusion, that a meeting between Fabian and Harry Drake was inevitable.

The deck was at this moment crowded with passengers and crew returning from service.

At half-past twelve the observation resulted in the following note:—

Lat. 40° 33′ N.

Long. 66° 24′ W.

Course, 214 miles.

Thus the "Great Eastern" was only 348 miles from Sandy Hook Point, a narrow tongue of land which forms the entrance to the New York harbour; it would not be long before we were in American seas.

I did not see Fabian in his usual place at lunch, but Drake was there, and although talkative, he did not appear to be quite at his ease. Was he trying to drown his fears in wine? I cannot say, but he indulged in bountiful libations with his friends. Several times I saw him leering at me, but insolent as he was, he dared not look me in the face. Was he looking for Fabian among the crowd of guests? I noticed he left the table abruptly before the meal was finished, and I got up immediately, in order to observe him, but he went to his cabin and shut himself up there

I went up on deck. Not a wave disturbed the calm surface of the sea, and the sky was unsullied by a cloud; the two mirrors mutually reflected their azure hue. I met Doctor Pitferge, who gave me bad news of the wounded sailor. The invalid was getting worse, and, in spite of the doctor's assurance, it was difficult to think that he could recover.

At four o'clock, a few minutes before dinner, a ship was hailed to larboard. The first officer told me he thought it must be the "City of Paris," one of the finest steamers of the "Inman Company," but he was mistaken, for the steamer coming nearer, sent us her name, which was the "Saxonia," belonging to the "National Steamship Company." For a few minutes the two boats came alongside, within two or three cables' length of each other. The deck of the "Saxonia" was covered with passengers, who saluted us with loud cheers.

At five o'clock another ship on the horizon, but too far off for her nationality to be recognized. This time it was undoubtedly the "City of Paris." This meeting with ships, and the salutation between the Atlantic's visitors, caused great excitement on board. One can understand that as there is little difference between one ship and another, the common danger of facing the uncertain element unites even strangers by a friendly bond.

At six o'clock a third ship appeared, the "Philadelphia," one of the Inman line, used for the transportation of emigrants from Liverpool to New York. We were evidently in frequented seas, and land could not be far off. How I longed to reach it!

The "Europe," a steamer belonging to the "Transatlantic

Company," carrying passengers from Havre to New York, was expected, but she did not come in sight, and had most likely taken a more northerly course.

Night closed in about half-past seven. As the sun sank below the horizon, the moon grew brighter and for some time hung shining in the heavens. A prayer-meeting, held by Captain Anderson, interspersed with hymns, lasted until nine o'clock.

The day passed without either Captain Corsican or myself receiving a visit from Drake's seconds.

CHAPTER XXIX.

THE next day, Monday, the 8th of April, the weather was very fine. I found the Doctor on deck basking in the sun. He came up to me. "Ah well!" said he, "our poor sufferer died in the night. The doctor never gave him up—oh, those doctors! they never will give in. This is the fourth man we have lost since we left Liverpool, the fourth gone towards paying the 'Great Eastern's' debt, and we are not at the end of our voyage yet."

"Poor fellow," said I, "just as we are nearing port, and the American coast almost in sight. What will become of his widow and little children?"

"Would you have it otherwise, my dear sir. It is the law, the great law! we must die! We must give way to others. It is my opinion we die simply because we are occupying a place which by rights belongs to another. Now can you tell me how many people will have died during my existence if I live to be sixty?"

"I have no idea, Doctor."

"The calculation is simple enough," resumed Dean Pitferge. "If I live sixty years, I shall have been in the world 21,900 days, or 525,600 hours, or 31,536,000 minutes, or lastly, 1,892,160,000 seconds, in round numbers 2,000,000,000 seconds. Now in that time two thousand millions individuals who were in the way of their successors will have died, and when I have become inconvenient, I shall be put out of the way in the same manner, so that the long and short of the matter is to put off becoming inconvenient as long as possible."

The Doctor continued for some time arguing on this subject, tending to prove to me a very simple theory, the mortality of human creatures. I did not think it worth while to discuss the point with him, so I let him have his say. Whilst we paced backwards and forwards, the Doctor talking, and I listening, I noticed that the carpenters on board were busy repairing the battered stem. If Captain Anderson did not wish to arrive in New York with damages, the carpenters would have to hurry over their work, for the "Great Eastern" was rapidly speeding through the tranquil waters; this I understood from the lively demeanour of the young lovers, who no longer thought of counting the turns of the wheels. The long pistons expanded, and the enormous cylinders heaving on their axle-swings, looked like a great peal of bells clanging together at random. The wheels made eleven revolutions a minute, and the steam-ship went at the rate of thirteen miles an hour.

At noon the officers dispensed with making an observation; they knew their situation by calculation, and land must be signalled before long.

While I was walking on deck after lunch, Captain Corsican came up. I saw, from the thoughtful expression on his face, that he had something to tell me.

" Fabian," said he, "has received Drake's seconds. I am to be his second, and he begs me to ask you if you would kindly be present on the occasion. He may rely on you?"

" Yes, Captain ; so all hope of deferring or preventing this meeting has vanished ?"

" All hope."

" But tell me, how did the quarrel arise ?"

" A discussion about the play was a pretext for it, nothing else. The fact is if Fabian was not aware who Harry Drake was, it is quite evident he knew Fabian, and the name of Fabian is so odious to him that he would gladly slay the man to whom it belongs."

" Who are Drake's seconds ?" I asked.

" One of them is that actor—"

" Doctor T—— ? "

" Just so ; the other is a Yankee I do not know."

"When are you to expect them?"

"I am waiting for them here."

And just as he spoke I saw the seconds coming towards us. Doctor T—— cleared his throat; he undoubtedly thought a great deal more of himself as the representative of a rogue. His companion, another of Drake's associates, was one of those extraordinary merchants who has always for sale anything you may ask him to buy.

Doctor T—— spoke first, after making a very emphatic bow, which Captain Corsican hardly condescended to acknowledge.

"Gentlemen," said Doctor T——, in a grave tone, "our friend Drake, a gentleman whose merit and deportment cannot fail to be appreciated by every one, has sent us to arrange a somewhat delicate affair with you; that is to say, Captain Fabian Mac Elwin, to whom we first addressed ourselves, referred us to you as his representative. I hope that we shall be able to come to an understanding between ourselves worthy the position of gentlemen touching the delicate object of our mission."

We made no reply, but allowed the gentleman to become embarrassed with his delicacy.

"Gentlemen," continued he, "there is not the remotest doubt but that Captain Mac Elwin is in the wrong. That gentleman has unreasonably, and without the slightest pretext, questioned the honour of Harry Drake's pro-

ceedings in a matter of play, and without any provoca-
tion offered him the greatest insult a gentleman could
receive."

These honeyed words made the Captain impatient, he
bit his moustache, and could refrain speaking no longer.

"Come to the point," said he sharply to Doctor T——,
whose speech he.had interrupted, "we don't want so many
words; the affair is simple enough; Captain Mac Elwin
raised his hand against Mr. Drake, your friend accepted
the blow, he assumes the part of the offended, and demands satisfaction. He has the choice of arms. What
next?"

"Does Captain Mac Elwin accept the challenge?" asked
the Doctor, baffled by Corsican's tone.

"Decidedly."

"Our friend, Harry Drake, has chosen swords."

"Very well, and where is the engagement to take place?
In New York?"

"No, here on board."

"On board, be it so; at what time? To-morrow
morning?"

"This evening at six o'clock, at the end of the upper-
deck, which will be deserted at that time."

"Very well."

Thus saying, the Captain took my arm, and turned his
back on Dr. T——.

CHAPTER XXX.

IT was no longer possible to put off the duel. Only a few hours separated us from the moment when Fabian and Harry Drake must meet. What could be the reason of this haste? How was it that Harry Drake had not delayed the duel until he and his enemy had disembarked? Was it because this ship, freighted by a French company, seemed to him the most favourable ground for a meeting which must be a deadly struggle? Or rather, might not Drake have a secret interest in freeing himself of Fabian before the latter could set foot on the American continent, or suspect the presence of Ellen on board, which he must have thought was unknown to all save himself? Yes, it must have been for this reason.

"Little matter, after all," said the Captain; "far better to have it over."

"Shall I ask Dr. Pitferge to be present at the duel as a doctor?"

l.

" Yes, it would be well to do so."

Corsican left me to go to Fabian. At this moment the bell on deck began tolling, and when I inquired of a steersman the reason of this unusual occurrence, he told me that it was for the burial of the sailor who had died in the night, and that the sad ceremony was about to take place. The sky, until now so clear, became overcast, and dark clouds loomed threateningly in the south.

At the sound of the bell the passengers flocked to the starboard side. The bridges, paddle-boards, bulwarks, masts and shore boats, hanging from their davits, were crowded with spectators, the officers, sailors, and stokers off duty, stood in ranks on deck.

At two o'clock a group of sailors appeared at the far end of the upper deck, they had left the hospital, and were passing the rudder-engine. The corpse, sewn in a piece of sail and stretched on a board, with a cannon ball at the feet, was carried by four men. The body, covered with the British flag, and followed by the dead man's comrades, slowly advanced into the midst of the spectators, who uncovered their heads as the procession passed.

On their arrival at the starboard paddle-wheel, the corpse was deposited on a landing of a staircase which terminated at the main deck.

In front of the row of spectators, standing one above the other, were Captain Anderson and his principal officers

THE PRAYER FOR THE DEAD.

Page 147.

in full uniform. The Captain, holding a prayer-book in his hand, took his hat off, and for some minutes, during a profound silenc., which not even the breeze interrupted, he solemnly read the prayer for the dead, every word of which was distinctly audible in the deathlike silence.

On a sign from the Captain the body, released by the bearers, sank into the sea. For one moment it floated on the surface, became upright, and then disappeared in a circle of foam.

At this moment the voice of the sailor on watch was heard crying "Land !"

CHAPTER XXXI.

THE land announced at the moment when the sea was closing over the corpse of the poor sailor was low-lying and of a yellow colour. This line of slightly elevated downs was Long Island, a great sandy bank enlivened with vegetation, which stretches along the American coast from Montauk Point to Brooklyn, adjoining New York. Several yachts were coasting along this island, which is covered with villas and pleasure-houses, the favourite resorts of the New Yorkists.

Every passenger waved his hand to the land so longed for after the tedious voyage, which had not been exempt from painful accidents. Every telescope was directed towards this first specimen of the American continent, and each saw it under a different aspect. The Yankee beheld in it his mother-land; the Southerner regarded these northern lands with a kind of scorn, the scorn of the conquered for the conqueror; the Canadian looked upon it as a man who had only one step to take to call himself a citizen of the Union ; the Californian in his mind's eye traversed the plains of the Far West, and crossing the Rocky Mountains had already set foot on their inexhaustible mines. The Mormonite, with elevated brow and scornful lip, hardly noticed these shores, but peered beyond to where stood the City of the Saints on the borders of Salt Lake, in the far-off deserts. As for the young lovers, this continent was to them the Promised Land.

In the meanwhile the sky was growing more and more threatening. A dark line of clouds gathered in the zenith, and a suffocating heat penetrated the atmosphere as though a July sun was shining directly above us.

" Would you like me to astonish you ? " said the Doctor, who had joined me on the gangway.

" Astonish me, Doctor ? "

" Well, then, we shall have a storm, perhaps a thunder-storm, before the day is over."

" A thunder-storm in the month of April ! " I cried.

" The ' Great Eastern ' does not trouble herself about seasons," replied Dean Pitferge, shrugging his shoulders. " It is a tempest called forth expressly on her account. Look at the threatening aspect of those clouds which cover the sky ; they look like antediluvian animals, and before long they will devour each other."

" I confess," said I, " the sky looks stormy, and were it

three months later I should be of your opinion, but not at this time of year."

"I tell you," replied the Doctor, growing animated, "the storm will burst out before many hours are past. I feel it like a barometer. Look at those vapours rising in a mass, observe that cirrus, those mares' tails which are blending together, and those thick circles which surround the horizon. Soon there will be a rapid condensing of vapour, which will consequently produce electricity. Besides the mercury has suddenly fallen, and the prevailing wind is south-west, the only one which can brew a storm in winter."

"Your observations may be very true, Doctor," said I, not willing to yield, "but who has ever witnessed a thunder-storm at this season, and in this latitude?"

"We have proof, sir, we have proof on record. Mild winters are often marked by storms. You ought only to have lived in 1172, or even in 1824, and you would have heard the roaring of the thunder, in the first instance in February, and in the second in December. In the month of January, 1837, a thunder-bolt fell near Drammen in Norway, and did considerable mischief. Last year, in the month of February, fishing-smacks from Tréport were struck by lightning. If I had time to consult statistics I would soon put you to silence."

"Well, Doctor, since you will have it so, we shall soon see. At any rate, you are not afraid of thunder?"

"Not I," replied the Doctor. "The thunder is my friend ; better still, it is my doctor."

"Your doctor ?"

"Most certainly. I was struck by lightning in my bed on the 13th July, 1867, at Kew, near London, and it cured me of paralysis in my right arm, when the doctors had given up the case as hopeless."

"You must be joking."

"Not at all. It is an economical treatment by electricity. My dear sir, there are many very authentic facts which prove that thunder surpasses the most skilful physicians, and its intervention is truly marvellous in apparently hopeless cases."

"Nevertheless," said I, "I have little trust in your doctor, and would not willingiy consult him."

"Because you have never seen him at work. Stay ; here is an instance which I have heard of as occurring in 1817. A peasant in Connecticut, who was suffering from asthma, supposed to be incurable, was struck by lightning in a field, and radically cured."

In fact I believe the Doctor would have been capable of making the thunder into pills.

"Laugh, ignoramus !" said he to me. "You know nothing either of the weather or medicine !"

CHAPTER XXXII.

DEAN PITFERGE left me, but I remained on deck, watching the storm rise. Corsican was still closeted with Fabian, who was undoubtedly making some arrangements in case of misfortune. I then remembered that he had a sister in New York, and I shuddered at the thought that perhaps we should have to carry to her the news of her brother's death. I should like to have seen Fabian, but I thought it better not to disturb either him or Captain Corsican.

At four o'clock we came in sight of land stretching before Long Island. It was Fire Island. In the centre rose a lighthouse, which shone over the surrounding land. The passengers again invaded the upper decks and bridges. All eyes were strained towards the coast, distant about six miles. They were waiting for the moment when the arrival of the pilot should settle the great pool business. It may be thought that those who had night quarters, and

I REMAINED ON DECK WATCHING THE STORM RISE.

Page 152

A SMALL SCHOONER WAS SIGNALLED TO STARBOARD.

Page 153.

I was of the number, had given up all pretensions, and that those with the day quarters, except those included between four and six o'clock, had no longer any chance. Before night the pilot would come on board and settle this affair, so that all the interest was now concentrated in the seven or eight persons to whom fate had attributed the next quarters. The latter were taking advantage of their good luck—selling, buying, and reselling their chances, bartering with such energy one might almost have fancied oneself in the Royal Exchange.

At sixteen minutes past four a small schooner, bearing towards the steam-ship, was signalled to starboard. There was no longer any possible doubt of its being the pilot's boat, and he would be on board in fourteen or fifteen minutes at the most. The struggle was now between the possessors of the second and third quarters from four to five o'clock. Demands and offers were made with renewed vivacity. Then absurd wagers were laid even on the pilot's person, the tenor of which I have faithfully given.

" Ten dollars that the pilot is married."

" Twenty that he is a widower."

" Thirty dollars that he has a moustache."

"Sixty that he has a wart on his nose."

" A hundred dollars that he will step on board with his right foot first."

" He will smoke."

" He will have a pipe in his mouth."

"No! a cigar."

"No!" "Yes!" "No!"

And twenty other wagers quite as ridiculous, which found those more absurd still to accept them.

In the meanwhile the little schooner was sensibly approaching the steam-ship, and we could distinguish her graceful proportions. These charming little pilot-boats, of about fifty or sixty tons, are good sea-boats, skimming over the water like sea-gulls. The schooner, gracefully inclined, was bearing windward in spite of the breeze, which had begun to freshen. Her mast and foresails stood out clearly against the dark background of clouds, and the sea foamed beneath her bows. When at two cables' length from the "Great Eastern," she suddenly veered and launched a shore-boat. Captain Anderson gave orders to heave-to, and for the first time during a fortnight the wheels of the screw were motionless. A man got into the boat, which four sailors quickly pulled to the steam-ship. A rope ladder was thrown over the side of the giant down to the pilot in his little nutshell, which the latter caught, and, skilfully climbing, sprang on deck.

He was received with joyous cries by the winners, and exclamations of disappointment from the losers. The pool was regulated by the following statements :—

" The pilot was married."

" He had no wart on his nose."

" He had a light moustache."

" He had jumped on board with both feet."

" Lastly, it was thirty-six minutes past four o'clock when he set foot on the deck of the ' Great Eastern.' "

The possessor of the thirty-third quarter thus gained the ninety-six dollars, and it was Captain Corsican, who had hardly thought of the unexpected gain. It was not long before he appeared on deck, and when the pool was presented to him, he begged Captain Anderson to keep it for the widow of the young sailor whose death had been caused by the inroad of the sea. The Captain shook his hand without saying a word, but a moment afterwards a sailor came up to Corsican, and, bowing awkwardly, " Sir," said he, " my mates have sent me to say that you are a very kind gentleman, and they all thank you in the name of poor Wilson, who cannot thank you for himself."

The Captain, moved by the rough sailor's speech, silently pressed his hand.

As for the pilot, he was a man of short stature, with not much of the sailor-look about him. He wore a glazed hat, black trousers, a brown overcoat lined with red, and carried an umbrella. He was master on board now.

In springing on deck, before he went to the bridge, he

had thrown a bundle of papers among the passengers, who eagerly pounced on them. They were European and American journals—the political and civil bonds whicn again united the "Great Eastern" to the two continents.

CHAPTER XXXIII.

THE storm was gathering, and a black arch of clouds had
formed over our heads; the atmosphere was misty; nature
was evidently about to justify Dr. Pitferge's presentiments
The steam-ship had slackened her speed, and the wheels
only made three or four revolutions a minute; volumes
of white steam escaped from the half-open valves, the
anchor-chains were cleared, and the British flag floated
from the mainmast; these arrangements Captain Anderson
had made preparatory to mooring. The pilot, standing on
the top of the starboard paddle, guided the steam-ship
through the narrow passages; but the tide was already
turning, so that the "Great Eastern" could not yet cross
the bar of the Hudson, and we must wait till next day.

At a quarter to five by the pilot's order the anchors were
let go; the chains rattled through the hawse-holes with a
noise like thunder. I even thought for a moment that the
storm had burst forth. When the anchors were firmly
embedded in the sand, the "Great Eastern" swung round

by the ebb tide, remained motionless, and not a wave disturbed the surface of the water.

At this moment the steward's trumpet sounded for the last time; it called the passengers to their farewell dinner. The "Society of Freighters" would be prodigal with the champagne, and no one wished to be absent. An hour later the saloons were crowded with guests, and the deck deserted.

However, seven persons left their places unoccupied; the two adversaries, who were going to stake their lives in a duel, the four seconds, and the Doctor, who was to be present at the engagement. The time and the place for the meeting had been well chosen; there was not a creature on deck; the passengers were in the dining-rooms, the sailors in their berths, the officers absorbed with their own particular bottles, and not a steersman on board, for the ship was motionless at anchor.

At ten minutes past five the Doctor and I were joined by Fabian and Captain Corsican. I had not seen Fabian since the scene in the smoking-room. He seemed to me sad, but very calm. The thought of the duel troubled him little, apparently; his mind was elsewhere, and his eyes wandered restlessly in search of Ellen. He held out his hand to me without saying a word.

"Has not Harry Drake arrived?" asked the Captain of me.

" Not yet," I replied.

" Let us go to the stern ; that is the place of rendezvous."

Fabian, Captain Corsican, and I, walked along the upper decks; the sky was growing dark ; we heard the distant roar of thunder rumbling along the horizon. It was like a monotonous bass, enlivened by the hips and hurrahs issuing from the saloons; flashes of lightning darted through the biack clouds, and the atmosphere was power-fully charged with electricity.

At twenty minutes past five Harry Drake and his seconds made their appearance. The gentlemen bowed to us, which honour we strictly returned. Drake did not utter a word, but his face showed signs of ill-concealed excitement. He cast a look of malignant hatred on Fabian ; but the latter, leaning against the hatchway, did not even see him ; so absorbed was he in a profound medi-tation, he seemed not yet to have thought of the part he was to play in this drama.

In the meanwhile Captain Corsican, addressing himself to the Yankee, one of Drake's seconds, asked him for the swords, which the latter presented to him. They were battle swords, the basket-hilts of which entirely protected the hand which held them. Corsican took them, bent, and measured them, and then allowed the Yankee to choose Whilst these preparations were being made, Harry Drake had taken off his hat and jacket, unbuttoned his shirt, and turned up his sleeves; then he seized his sword, and I saw that he was left-handed, which gave him, accustomed to right-handed antagonists, an unquestionable advantage.

Fabian had not yet left the place where he was standing. One would have thought that these preparations had nothing to do with him. Captain Corsican went up to him, touched him, and showed him the sword. Fabian looked at the glittering steel, and it seemed as if his memory came back to him at that moment.

He grasped his sword with a firm hand.

" Right !" he murmured ; " I remember !"

Then he placed himself opposite Harry Drake, who immediately assumed the defensive.

" Proceed, gentlemen," said the Captain.

They immediately crossed swords. From the first clashing of steel, several rapid passes on both sides, certain extrications, parries, and thrusts proved to me the equality in strength of the opponents. I augured well for Fabian. He was cool, self-possessed, and almost indifferent to the struggle; certainly less affected by it than were his own seconds. Harry Drake, on the contrary, scowled at him with flashing eyes and clenched teeth, his head bent forward, and his whole countenance indicative of a hatred which deprived him of all composure. He had come there to kill, and kill he would.

After the first engagement, which lasted some minutes, swords were lowered. With the exception of a slight scratch on Fabian's arm, neither of the combatants had been wounded. They rested, and Drake wiped off the perspiration with which his face was bathed.

The storm now burst forth in all its fury. The thunder was continuous, and broke out in loud deafening reports; the atmosphere was charged with electricity to such an extent that the swords were gilded with luminous crests, like lightning conductors in the midst of thunder clouds.

After a few moments' rest, Corsican again gave the signal to proceed, and Fabian and Harry Drake again fell to work.

This time the fight was much more animated ; Fabian defending himself with astounding calmness, Drake madly attacking him. Several times I expected a stroke from Fabian, which was not even attempted.

Suddenly, after some quick passes, Drake made a rapid stroke. I thought that Fabian must have been struck in the chest, but, warding off the blow, he struck Harry Drake's sword smartly. The latter raised and covered himself by a swift semi-circle ; whilst the lightning rent the clouds overhead.

Suddenly, and without anything to explain this strange surrender of himself, Fabian dropped his sword. Had he been mortally wounded without our noticing it ? The

M

blood rushed wildly to my heart. Fabian's eyes had grown singularly animated.

"Defend yourself," roared Drake, drawing himself up like a tiger ready to spring on to his prey.

I thought that it was all over with Fabian, disarmed as he was. Corsican threw himself between him and his enemy, to prevent the latter from striking a defenceless man; but now Harry Drake in his turn stood motionless.

I turned, and saw Ellen, pale as death, her hands stretched out, coming towards the duellists. Fabian, fascinated by this apparition, remained perfectly still.

"You! you!" cried Harry Drake to Ellen; "you here!"

His uplifted blade gleamed as though on fire; one might have said it was the sword of the archangel Michael in the hands of a demon.

Suddenly a brilliant flash of lightning lit up the whole stern. I was almost knocked down, and felt suffocated, for the air was filled with sulphur; but by a powerful effort I regained my senses.

I had fallen on one knee, but I got up and looked around. Ellen was leaning on Fabian. Harry Drake seemed petrified, and remained in the same position, but his face had grown black.

Had the unhappy man been struck when attracting the lightning with his blade?

Ellen left Fabian, and went up to Drake with her face

I TURNED, AND SAW ELLEN, PALE AS DEATH

Page 162

full of holy compassion. She placed her hand on his shoulder; even this light touch was enough to disturb the equilibrium, and Drake fell to the ground a corpse.

Ellen bent over the body, whilst we drew back terrified. The wretched Harry Drake was dead.

"Struck by lightning," said Dean Pitferge, catching hold of my arm. "Struck by lightning! Ah! will you not now believe in the intervention of thunder?"

Had Harry Drake indeed been struck by lightning as Dean Pitferge affirmed, or rather, as the doctor on board said, had a blood-vessel broken in his chest? I can only say there was nothing now but a corpse before our eyes.

CHAPTER XXXIV.

THE next day, Tuesday, the 9th of April, the "Great Eastern" weighed anchor, and set sail to enter the Hudson, the pilot guiding her with an unerring eye. The storm had spent itself in the night, and the last black clouds disappeared below the horizon. The aspect of the sea was enlivened by a flotilla of schooners, waiting along the coast for the breeze.

A small steamer came alongside, and we were boarded by the officer of the New York sanitary commissioners.

It was not long before we passed the light-boat which marks the channels of the Hudson, and ranged near Sandy Hook Point, where a group of spectators greeted us with a volley of hurrahs.

When the "Great Eastern" had gone round the interior bay formed by Sandy Hook Point, through the flotilla of fishing-smacks, I caught a glimpse of the verdant heights of New Jersey, the enormous forts on the bay, then the low line of the great city stretching between the Hudson and East river.

In another hour, after having ranged opposite the New York quays, the "Great Eastern" was moored in the Hudson, and the anchors became entangled in the submarine cable, which must necessarily be broken on her departure.

Then began the disembarkation of all my fellow-voyagers whom I should never see again : Californians, Southerners, Mormonites, and the young lovers. I was waiting for Fabian and Corsican.

I had been obliged to inform Captain Anderson of the incidents relating to the duel which had taken place on board. The doctors made their report, and nothing whatever having been found wrong in the death of Harry Drake, orders were given that the last duties might be rendered to him on land.

At this moment Cockburn, the statician, who had not spoken to me the whole of the voyage, came up and said,—

"Do you know, sir, how many turns the wheels have made during our passage?"

"I do not, sir."

"One hundred thousand, seven hundred and twenty-three."

"Ah! really sir, and the screw?"

"Six hundred and eight thousand, one hundred and thirty."

"I am much obliged to you, sir, for the information."

And the statician left me without any farewell whatever

Fabian and Corsican joined me at this moment. Fabian pressed my hand warmly.

"Ellen," said he to me, "Ellen will recover. Her reason came back to her for a moment. Ah! God is just, and He will restore her wholly to us."

Whilst thus speaking, Fabian smiled as he thought of the future. As for Captain Corsican, he kissed me heartily without any ceremony.

"Good-bye, good-bye, we shall see you again," he cried to me, when he had taken his place in the tender where were Fabian and Ellen, under the care of Mrs. R——, Captain Mac Elwin's sister, who had come to meet her brother.

Then the tender sheered off, taking the first convoy of passengers to the Custom House pier.

I watched them as they went farther and farther away, and, seeing Ellen sitting between Fabian and his sister, I could not doubt that care, devotion, and love would restore to this poor mind the reason of which grief had robbed it.

Just then some one took hold of my arm, and I knew it was Dr. Pitferge.

"Well," said he, "and what is going to become of you?"

"My idea was, Doctor, since the 'Great Eastern' remains a hundred and ninety-two hours at New York, and as I must return with her, to spend the hundred and ninety-two hours in America. Certainly it is but a week, but a week well spent is, perhaps, long enough to see New York, the Hudson, the Mohawk Valley, Lake Erie, Niagara, and all the country made familiar by Cooper.

"Ah! you are going to the Niagara!" cried Dean Pitferge. "I'll declare I should not be sorry to see it again, and if my proposal does not seem very disagreeable to you—"

The worthy Doctor amused me with his crotchets. I had taken a fancy to him, and here was a well-instructed guide placed at my service.

"That's settled, then," said I to him.

A quarter of an hour later we embarked on the tender and at three o'clock were comfortably lodged in two rooms of Fifth Avenue Hotel.

CHAPTER XXXV.

A WEEK to spend in America ! The "Great Eastern" was
to set sail on the 16th of April, and it was now the 9th,
and three o'clock in the afternoon, when I set foot on the
land of the Union. A week ! There are furious tourists
and express travellers who would probably find this time
enough to visit the whole of North America ; but I had no
such pretention, not even to visit New York thoroughly, and
to write, after this extra rapid inspection, a book on the
manners and customs of the Americans. But the consti-
tution and physical aspect of New York is soon seen ; it
is hardly more varied than a chess-board. The streets, cut
at right angles, are called avenues when they are straight,
and streets when irregular. The numbers on the principal thoroughfares are a very practical but monotonous
arrangement. American cars run through all the avenues.
Any one who has seen one quarter of New York knows
the whole of the great city, except, perhaps, that intricacy

of streets and confused alleys appropriated by the commercial population.

New York is built on a tongue of land, and all its activity is centred on the end of that tongue; on either side extend the Hudson and East River, arms of the sea, in fact, on which ships are seen and ferry-boats ply, connecting the town on the right hand with Brooklyn, and on the left with the shores of New Jersey.

A single artery intersects the symmetrical quarters of New York, and that is old Broadway, the Strand of London, and the Boulevard Montmatre of Paris ; hardly passable at its lower end, where it is crowded with people, and almost deserted higher up ; a street where sheds and marble palaces are huddled together ; a stream of carriages, omnibusses, cabs, drays, and waggons, with the pavement for its banks, across which a bridge has been thrown for the traffic of foot passengers. Broadway is New York, and it was there that the Doctor and I walked until evening.

After having dined at Fifth Avenue Hotel, I ended my day's work by going to the Barnum Theatre, where they were acting a play called "New York Streets," which attracted a large audience. In the fourth Act there was a fire, and real fire-engines, worked by real firemen ; hence the "great attraction."

The next morning I left the Doctor to his own affairs, and agreed to meet him at the hotel at two o'clock. My first proceeding was to go to the Post Office, 51, Liberty Street, to get any letters awaiting me there; then I went to No. 2, Bowling Green, at the bottom of Broadway, the residence of the French consul, M. le Baron Gauldrée Boilleau, who received me very kindly. From here I made my way to cash a draft at Hoffman's; lastly, I went to No. 25, Thirty-sixth Street, where resided Mrs. R——, Fabian's sister. I was impatient to get news of Ellen and my two friends; and here I learnt that, following the Doctor's advice, Mrs. R——, Fabian, and Corsican had left New York, taking with them the young lady, thinking that the air and quiet of the country might have a beneficial effect on her. A line from Captain Corsican informed me of this sudden departure. The kind fellow had been to Fifth Avenue Hotel without meeting me, but he promised to keep me acquainted with their whereabouts. They thought of stopping at the first place that attracted Ellen's attention, and, staying there as long as the charm lasted; he hoped that I should not leave without bidding them a last farewell. Yes, were it but for a few hours, I should be happy to see Ellen, Fabian, and Corsican once again. But such are the drawbacks of travelling, hurried as I was, they gone and I going, each our separate ways, it seemed hardly likely I should see them again.

At two o'clock I returned to the hotel, and found the

Doctor in the bar-room, which was full of people. It is a public hall, where travellers and passers-by mingled together, finding gratis iced-water, biscuits, and cheese.

" Well, Doctor," said I, " when shall we start ?"

" At six o'clock this evening."

" Shall we take the Hudson railroad?"

" No; the 'St. John ;' a wonderful steamer, another world—a 'Great Eastern' of the river, one of those admirable locomotive engines which go along with a will. I should have preferred showing you the Hudson by daylight, but the 'St. John' only goes at night. To-morrow, at five o'clock in the morning, we shall be at Albany. At six o'clock we shall take the New York Central Railroad, and in the evening we shall sup at Niagara Falls."

I did not discuss the Doctor's programme, but accepted it willingly.

The hotel lift hoisted us .to our rooms, and some minutes later we descended with our tourist knapsacks. A fly took us in a quarter of an hour to the pier on the Hudson, before which was the " St. John," the chimneys of which were already crowned with wreaths of smoke.

CHAPTER XXXVI.

THE " St. John," and its sister ship, the " Dean Richmond," are two of the finest steam-ships on the river. They are buildings rather than boats; terraces rise one above another, with galleries and verandahs. One would almost have thought it was a gardener's floating plantation. There are twenty flag-staffs, fastened with iron tressings, which consolidate the whole building. The two enormous paddle-boxes are painted *al fresco*, like the tympans in the Church of St. Mark, at Venice. Behind each wheel rises the chimney of the two boilers, the latter placed outside, instead of in the hull of the steam-ship, a good precaution in case of explosion. In the centre, between the paddles, is the machinery, which is very simple, consisting only of a single cylinder, a piston worked by a long cross-beam, which rises and falls like the monstrous hammer of a forge, and a single crank, communicating the movement to the axles of the massive wheels.

Passengers were already crowding on to the deck of the "St. John." Dean Pitferge and I went to secure a cabin; we got one which opened into an immense saloon, a kind of gallery with a vaulted ceiling, supported by a succession of Corinthian pillars. Comfort and luxury everywhere, carpets, sofas, ottomans, paintings, mirrors, even gas, made in a small gasometer on board.

At this moment the gigantic engine trembled and began to work. I went on to the upper terraces. At the stern was a gaily painted house, which was the steersman's room, where four strong men stood at the spokes of the double rudder-wheel. After walking about for a few minutes, I went down on to the deck, between the already heated boilers, from which light blue flames were issuing. Of the Hudson I could see nothing. Night came, and with it a fog thick enough to be cut. The "St. John" snorted in the gloom like a true mastodon; we could hardly catch a glimpse of the lights of the towns scattered along the banks of the river, or the lanterns of ships ascending the dark water with shrill whistles.

At eight o'clock I went into the saloon. The Doctor took me to have supper at a magnificent restaurant placed between the decks, where we were served by an army of black waiters. Dean Pitferge informed me that the number of passengers on board was more than four thousand, reckoning fifteen hundred emigrants stowed away in the lower part of the steam-ship. Supper finished, we retired to our comfortable cabin.

At eleven o'clock I was aroused by a slight shock. The "St. John" had stopped. The captain, finding it impossible to proceed in the darkness, had given orders to heave-to, and the enormous boat, moored in the channel, slept tranquilly at anchor.

At four o'clock in the morning the "St. John" resumed her course. I got up and went out under one of the verandahs. The rain had ceased, the fog cleared off, the water appeared, then the shores; the right bank, dotted with green trees and shrubs, which gave it the appearance of a long cemetery; in the background rose high hills, closing in the horizon by a graceful line; the left bank, on the contrary, was flat and marshy.

Dr. Pitferge had just joined me under the verandah.

"Good morning, friend," said he, after having drawn a good breath of air; "do you know we shall not be at Albany in time to catch the train, thanks to that wretched fog. This will modify my programme."

"So much the worse, Doctor, for we must be economical with our time."

"Right; we may expect to reach Niagara Falls at night instead of in the evening. That is not my fault, but we must be resigned."

The "St. John," in fact, did not moor off the Albany

THE FOG CLEARED OFF.

Page 114

quay before eight o'clock. The train had left, so we were
obliged to wait till half-past one. In consequence of this
delay we were able to visit the curious old city, which forms
the legislative centre of the State of New York: the
lower town, commercial and thickly populated, on the right
bank of the Hudson, and the high town, with its brick
houses, public buildings, and its very remarkable museum
of fossils. One might almost have thought it a large quarter of New York transported to the side of this hill, up
which it rises in the shape of an amphitheatre.

At one o'clock, after having breakfasted, we went to the
station, which was without any barrier or officials. The
train simply stopped in the middle of the street, like an
omnibus ; one could get up and down at pleasure. The cars
communicate with each other by bridges, which allow the
traveller to go from one end of the train to the other. At
the appointed time, without seeing either a guard or a
porter, without a bell, without any warning, the brisk locomotive, a real gem of workmanship, started, and we were
whirled away at the speed of fifty miles an hour. But
instead of being boxed up, as one is in European trains,
we were at liberty to walk about, buy newspapers and books,
without waiting for stations. Refreshment buffets, book-
stalls, everything was at hand for the traveller. We
were now crossing fields without fences, and forests newly
cleared, at the risk of a collision with the felled trees ;

through new towns, seamed with rails, but still wanting in houses ; through cities adorned with the most poetic names of ancient literature—Rome, Syracuse, and Palmyra. It was thus the Mohawk Valley, the land of Fenimore, which belongs to the American novelist, as does the land of Rob Roy to Walter Scott, glided before our eyes. For a moment Lake Ontario, which Cooper has made the scene of action of his master-work, sparkled on the horizon. All this theatre of the grand epopee of Leather Stocking, formerly a savage country, is now a civilized land. The Doctor did not appreciate the change, for he persisted in calling me Hawk's Eye, and would only answer to the name of Chingachgook.

At eleven o'clock at night we changed trains at Rochester ; the spray from the Tennessee cascades fell over the cars in showers. At two o'clock in the morning, after having kept alongside the Niagara for several leagues without seeing it, we arrived at the village of Niagara Falls, and the Doctor conducted me to a magnificent hotel, grandly named "Cataract House."

CHAPTER XXXVII.

THE Niagara is not a stream, not even a river; it is simply a weir sluice, a canal thirty-six miles long, which empties the waters of the Lakes Superior, Michigan, Huron, and Erie into the Ontario. The difference in the level of these last two lakes is three hundred and forty feet; this difference uniformly proportioned the whole of the width would hardly have created a "rapid;" but the Falls alone absorb half the difference in level, whence their formidable power.

This Niagarine trench separates the United States from Canada. Its right bank is American and its left English; on one side policemen, on the other not the shadow of one.

On the morning of the 12th of April, at break of day, the Doctor and I walked down the wide street of Niagara Falls, which is the name of the village situated on the banks of the Falls. It is a kind of small watering-place, three hundred miles from Albany, built in a healthy and charming situation, provided with sumptuous hotels and

N

comfortable villas, which the Yankees and Canadians frequent in the season. The weather was magnificent, the sun warmed the cold atmosphere, a dull, distant roar was heard, and I saw vapours on the horizon which could not be clouds.

"Is that the Fall?" I asked of the Doctor.

"Patience!" replied Pitferge.

In a few minutes we were on the banks of the Niagara. The river was flowing peacefully along ; it was clear, and not deep, with numerous projections of grey rock emerging here and there. The roar of the cataract grew louder and louder, but as yet we could not see it. A wooden bridge, supported by iron arches, united the left bank to an island in the midst of the current ; on to this bridge the Doctor led me. Above, stretched the river as far as the eye could reach ; down the stream, that is to say on our right, the first unevenness of a rapid was noticeable ; then, at half a mile from the bridge, the earth suddenly gave way, and clouds of spray filled the air. This was the American fall, which we could not see. Beyond, on the Canadian side, lay a peaceful country, with hills, villas, and bare trees.

"Don't look! don't look!" cried the Doctor to me; "reserve yourself, shut your eyes, and do not open them until I tell you!"

I hardly listened to my original, but continued to look. The bridge crossed. we set foot on the island known as

NATURE HAS COMBINED EVERYTHING TO ASTONISH THE EYE.

Page 179.

Goat Island. It is a piece of land of about seventy acres, covered with trees, and intersected with lovely avenues with carriage drives. It is like a bouquet thrown between the American and Canadian Falls, separated from the shore by a distance of three hundred yards. We ran under the great trees, climbed the slopes, and went down the steps; the thundering roar of the falls was redoubled, and the air saturated with spray.

"Look!" cried the Doctor.

Coming from behind a mass of rock, the Niagara appeared in all its splendour. At this spot it meets with a sharp angle of land, and falling round it, forms the Canadian cascade, called the "Horse-shoe Fall," which falls from a height of one hundred and fifty-eight feet, and is two miles broad.

In this, one of the most beautiful spots in the world, Nature has combined everything to astonish the eye. The fall of the Niagara singularly favours the effects of light and shade; the sunbeams falling on the water, capriciously diversify the colour; and those who have seen this effect, must admit that it is without parallel. In fact, near Goat Island the foam is white; it is then a fall of snow, or a heap of melted silver, pouring into the abyss. In the centre of the cataract the colour of the water is a most beautiful sea-green, which indicates its depth, so that the "Detroit," a ship drawing twenty feet and launched on the current, was able to descend the falls without grazing. Towards the Canadian shore the whirlpool, on the contrary, looks like metal shining beneath the luminous rays, and it is melted gold which is now poured into the gulf. Below, the river is invisible from the vapours which rise over it. I caught glimpses, however, of enormous blocks of ice accumulated by the cold of winter ; they take the form of monsters, which, with open jaws, hourly absorb the hundred millions of tons poured into them by the inexhaustible Niagara. Half a mile below the cataract the river again became tranquil, and presented a smooth surface, which the winds of April had not yet been able to ruffle.

"And now for the middle of the torrent," said the Doctor to me.

I could not imagine what the Doctor meant by those words, until he pointed to a tower built on the edge of a rock some hundred feet from the shore, almost overhanging the precipice. This monument, raised in 1833, by a certain audacious being, one Judge Porter, is called the "Terrapin Tower."

We went down the steps of Goat Island, and, coming to the height of the upper course of the Niagara, I saw a bridge, or rather some planks, thrown from one rock to the other, which united the tower with the banks of the river. The bridge was but a few feet from the abyss, and below it roared the torrent. We ventured on these planks, and in a few minutes reached the rock which supported Terrapin Tower. This round tower, forty-five feet in height, is built of stone, with a circular balcony at its summit, and a roof covered with red stucco. The winding staircase, on which thousands of names are cut, is wooden. Once at the top of the tower, there is nothing to do but cling to the balcony and look.

The tower is in the midst of the cataract. From its summit the eye plunges into the depths of the abyss, and peers into the very jaws of the ice monsters, as they swallow the torrent. One feels the rock tremble which supports it. It is impossible to hear anything but the roaring of the surging water. The spray rises to the top of the monument, and splendid rainbows are formed by the sun shining on the vapourized water.

By a simple optical illusion, the tower seems to move with a frightful rapidity, but, happily, in the opposite direction to the fall, for, with the contrary illusion, it would be impossible to look at the gulf from giddiness.

Breathless and shivering, we went for a moment inside the top landing of the tower, and it was then that the Doctor took the opportunity of saying to me,—

" This Terrapin Tower, my dear sir, will some day fall into the abyss, and perhaps sooner than is expected."

Ah ! indeed ! "

"There is no doubt about it. The great Canadian Fall recedes insensibly, but still, it recedes. The tower, when it was first built in 1833, was much farther from the cataract. Geologists say that the fall, in the space of thirty-five thousand years, will be found at Queenstown, seven miles up the stream. According to Mr. Bakewell, it recedes a yard in a year; but according to Sir Charles Lyell one foot only. The time will come when the rock which supports the tower, worn away by the water, will glide down the Falls of the cataract. Well, my dear sir, remember this: the day when the Terrapin Tower falls, there will be some eccentrics who will descend the Niagara with it."

I looked at the Doctor, as if to ask him if he would be of that number, but he signed for me to follow him, and we went out again to look at the "Horse-shoe Fall," and the surrounding country. We could now distinguish the American Fall, slightly curtailed and separated by a projection of the island, where there is another small central cataract one hundred feet wide; the American cascade, equally fine, falls perpendicularly. Its height is one hundred and sixty-four feet. But in order to have a good view of it it is necessary to stand facing it, on the Canadian side.

All day we wandered on the banks of the Niagara, irresistibly drawn back to the tower, where the roar of the water, the spray, the sunlight playing on the vapours, the excitement, and the briny odour of the cataract, holds you in a perpetual ecstasy. Then we went back to Goat Island to get the Fall from every point of view, without ever being wearied of looking at it. The Doctor would have taken me to see the "Grotto of Winds," hollowed out underneath the central Fall, but access to it was not allowed, on account of the frequent falling away of the rocks.

At five o'clock we went back to the hotel, and after a hasty dinner, served in the American fashion, we returned to Goat Island. The Doctor wished to go and see the "Three Sisters," charming little islets scattered at the head of the island ; then, with the return of evening, he led me back to the tottering rock of Terrapin Tower.

The last rays of the setting sun had disappeared behind the grey hills, and the moon shed her soft clear light over the landscape. The shadow of the tower stretched across the abyss ; farther down the stream the water glided silently along, crowned with a light mist. The Canadian shore, already plunged in darkness, contrasted vividly with the moon-lit banks of Goat Island, and the village of Niagara Falls. Below us, the gulf, magnified by the uncertain light, looked like a bottomless abyss. in which roared the formidable torrent. What effect ! What artist could ever depict such a scene, either with the pen or paint-brush ? For some minutes a moving light appeared on the horizon ; it was the signal light of a train crossing the Niagara bridge at a distance of two miles from us. Here we remained silent and motionless on the top of the tower until midnight, leaning over the waters which possessed such a fascination. Once, when the moon-beams caught the liquid dust at a certain angle, I had a glimpse of a milky band of transparent ribbon trembling in the shadows. It was a lunar rainbow, a pale irradiation of the queen of the night, whose soft light was refracted through the mist of the cataract.

CHAPTER XXXVIII.

THE next day, the 13th of April, the Doctor's programme announced a visit to the Canadian shore. We had only to follow the heights of the bank of the Niagara for two miles to reach the suspension bridge. We started at seven o'clock in the morning. From the winding path on the right bank we could see the tranquil waters of the river, which no longer felt the perturbation of its fall.

At half-past seven we reached the suspension bridge. It is the bridge, on which the Great Western and New York Central Railroads meet, and the only one which gives access to Canada on the confines of the State of New York. This suspension bridge is formed of two platforms; the upper one for trains, and the lower for carriages and pedestrians. Imagination seems to lose itself in contemplating this stupendous work. This viaduct, over which trains can pass, suspended at a height of two hundred and fifty feet above the Niagara, again transformed into a rapid at this spot. This suspension bridge, built by John A. Roebling, of Trendon (New Jersey), is eight hundred feet long, and twenty-four wide ; the iron props fastened to the shore prevent it from swinging ; the chains which support it, formed of four thousand wires, are ten inches in diameter, and can bear a weight of twelve thousand four hundred tons. The bridge itself weighs but eight hundred tons, and cost five hundred thousand dollars. Just as we reached the centre a train passed over our heads, and we felt the platform bend under its weight.

It is a little below this bridge that Blondin crossed the Niagara, on a rope stretched from one shore to the other, and not, as is generally supposed, across the falls. However, the undertaking was none the less perilous ; but if Blondin astonished us by his daring, what must we think of his friend who accompanied him, riding on his back during this aerial promenade ?

" Perhaps he was a glutton," said the Doctor, " and Blondin made wonderful omelets on his tight-rope."

We were now on Canadian ground, and we walked up the left bank of the Niagara, in order to see the Falls under a new aspect. Half an hour later we reached the English hotel, where the Doctor ordered our breakfast, whilst I glanced through the " Travellers' Book," where figured several thousand names : among the most celebrated I

THE CATARACT FALLING BEFORE US.

noticed the following:—Robert Peel, Lady Franklin, Comte de Paris, Duc de Chartres, Prince de Joinville, Louis Napoleon (1846), Prince and Princess Napoleon, Barnum (with his address), Maurice Sand (1865), Agassis (1854), Almonte, Prince Hohenlohe, Rothschild, Bertin (Paris), Lady Elgin, Burkhardt (1832), &c.

"And now let us go under the Falls," said the Doctor to me, when we had finished breakfast.

I followed Dean Pitferge. A negro conducted us to the dressing-room, where we were provided with waterproof trousers, macintoshes, and glazed hats. Thus equipped, our guide led us down a slippery path, obstructed by sharp-edged stones, to the lower level of the Niagara. Then we passed behind the great fall through clouds of spray, the cataract falling before us like the curtain of a theatre before the actors. But what a theatre! Soaked, blinded, deafened, we could neither see nor hear in this cavern as hermetically closed by the liquid sheets of the cataract as though Nature had sealed it in by a wall of granite.

At nine o'clock we returned to the hotel, where they relieved us of our streaming clothes. Going back again to the bank, I uttered a cry of surprise and joy,—

"Captain Corsican!"

The Captain heard, and came towards me.

"You here!" he cried; "what a pleasure to see you again!"

"And Fabian? and Ellen?" I asked, shaking both his hands.

"They are here, and going on as well as possible; Fabian full of hope, almost merry; and our poor Ellen little by little regaining reason."

"But how is it that I meet you at the Niagara?"

"The Niagara," repeated Corsican. "Well, it is the principal resort of English and Americans in the warm months. They come here to breathe, to be cured by the sublime spectacle of the Falls. Our Ellen seemed to be struck at first sight by this glorious scenery, and we have come to stay on the banks of the Niagara. You see that villa, 'Clifton House,' in the midst of those trees, half way up the hill; that is where we all live, with Mrs. R——, Fabian's sister, who is devoted to our poor friend."

"Has Ellen recognized Fabian?" I asked.

"No, not yet," replied the Captain. "You are aware, however, that at the moment when Drake was struck dead, Ellen had a brief interval of consciousness. Her reason became clear in the gloom which surrounded her, but this did not last long. At the same time, since we brought her to breathe this fresh air in this quiet place, the doctor has discovered a sensible improvement in her condition. She is calm, her sleep is tranquil, but there is a look in her eyes as though she were trying to think of something past or present."

" Ah," my dear friend !" cried I, " you will cure her ; but where are Fabian and his betrothed ? "

" Look !" said Corsican, and he pointed towards the shore of the Niagara.

In the direction indicated by the Captain I saw Fabian, who had not yet noticed us. He was standing on a rock, and a few feet in front of him sat Ellen perfectly motionless, Fabian watching her all the time. This spot on the left bank is known by the name of " Table Rock." It is a kind of rocky promontory jutting out into the river, which roars at a distance of four hundred feet below. Formerly it was more extensive, but the crumbling away of large pieces of rock has now reduced it to a surface a few yards square.

Ellen seemed absorbed in speechless ecstasy. From this place the aspect of the Falls is " most sublime," as say the guides, and they are right. It gives a view of two cataracts ; on the right the " Canadian Fall," the crest of which, crowned with vapours, shuts in the horizon on one side, like the horizon of the sea. In front is the " American Fall," and above, the elegant village of Niagara Falls, half hidden in the trees ; on the left, the whole perspective of the river flowing rapidly between its high banks, and below the torrent struggling against the overthrown icebergs.

Corsican, the Doctor, and I went towards Table Rock,

but I did not want to disturb Fabian. Ellen was as
motionless as a statue. What impression was this scene
making on her mind? Was reason gradually coming back
to her under the influence of the grand spectacle? Suddenly I saw Fabian step towards her. Ellen had risen
quickly, and was going near to the abyss, with her arms
extended towards the gulf; but all at once she stopped,
and passed her hand rapidly across her forehead, as if she
would drive away some thought. Fabian, pale as death,
but self-possessed, with one bound placed himself between
Ellen and the chasm; the latter shook back her fair hair,
and her graceful figure staggered. Did she see Fabian?
No. One would have said it was a dead person coming
back to being, and looking round for life!

Captain Corsican and I dared not move, although, being
so near the abyss, we dreaded some catastrophe; but the
Doctor kept us back.

"Let Fabian alone," said he.

I heard the sobs which escaped from the young woman's
heaving breast, the inarticulate words which came from her
lips; she seemed as though she were trying to speak, but
could not. At last she uttered these words:—

"My God! my God! where am I, where am I?"

"She was conscious that some one was near her, for she
half turned round, and her whole face seemed trans-
figured.

"FABIAN! FABIAN!" CRIED SHE, "AT LAST."

Page 191.

There was a new light in her eyes, as she saw Fabian, trembling and speechless, standing before her with out-stretched arms.

"Fabian! Fabian!" cried she, at last.

Fabian caught her in his arms, where she fell in an un-conscious state. He uttered a piercing cry, thinking that Ellen was dead, but the Doctor interposed.

"Don't be alarmed," said he; "this crisis, on the con-trary, will be the means of saving her!"

Ellen was carried to Clifton House and put to bed, where she recovered consciousness and slept peacefully.

Fabian, encouraged by the Doctor, was full of hope. Ellen had recognized him! Coming back to us, he said to me,—

"We shall save her, we shall save her! Every day I watch her coming back to life. To-day, to-morrow, per-haps she will be restored to me. Ah! the just God be praised! We will stay here as long as it is necessary for her, shall we not, Archibald?"

The Captain clasped Fabian in his arms; then the latter turned to the Doctor and me. He loaded us with thanks, and inspired us with the hope which filled his breast, and never was there better reason for hope—Ellen's recovery was near at hand.

But we must be starting, and there was hardly an hour for us to reach Niagara Falls. Ellen was still sleeping when we left our dear friends. Fabian and Corsican bid us a last farewell, after having promised we should have news of Ellen by telegram, and at noon we left Clifton House.

CHAPTER XXXIX.

SOME minutes later we were descending a long flight of
steps on the Canadian side, which led to the banks of the
river, covered with huge sheets of ice. Here a boat was
waiting to take us to "America." One passenger had
already taken his place in it. He was an engineer from
Kentucky, and acquainted the Doctor with his name and
profession. We embarked without loss of time, and by dint
of steering, so as to avoid the blocks of ice, reached the
middle of the river, where the current offered a clear passage. From here we had a last view of the magnificent
Niagara cataract. Our companion observed it with a
thoughtful air.

"Is it not grand, sir? Is it not magnificent?" said I to
him.

"Yes," replied he; "but what a waste of mechanical
force, and what a mill might be turned with such a fall as
that!"

Never did I feel more inclined to pitch an engineer into the water!

On the other bank a small and almost vertical railroad, worked by a rope on the American side, hoisted us to the top. At half-past one we took the express, which put us down at Buffalo at a quarter past two. After visiting this large new town, and tasting the water of Lake Erie, we again took the New York Central Railway at six o'clock in the evening. The next day, on leaving the comfortable beds of a "sleeping car," we found ourselves at Albany, and the Hudson Railroad, which runs along the left bank of the river, brought us to New York a few hours later.

The next day, the 15th of April, in company with the indefatigable Doctor, I went over the city, East River, and Brooklyn. In the evening I bade farewell to the good Dean Pitferge, and I felt, in leaving him, that I left a friend.

Tuesday, the 16th of April, was the day fixed for the departure of the "Great Eastern." At eleven o'clock I went to Thirty-seventh pier, where the tender was to await the passengers. It was already filled with people and luggage when I embarked. Just as the tender was leaving the quay some one caught hold of my arm, and turning round I saw Dr. Pitferge.

" You ! " I cried ; " and are you going back to Europe ? "

" Yes, my dear sir."

"By the 'Great Eastern'?"

"Undoubtedly," replied the amiable original, smiling; "I have considered the matter, and have come to the conclusion that I must go. Only think, this may be the 'Great Eastern's' *last voyage; the one which she will never complete*."

The bell for departure had rung, when one of the waiters from Fifth Avenue Hotel came running up to me, and put a telegram into my hands, dated from Niagara Falls:—"Ellen has awakened; her reason has entirely returned to her," said Captain Corsican, "and the doctor has every hope of her recovery."

I communicated this good news to Dean Pitferge.

"Every hope for her indeed! every hope!" said my fellow-traveller, in a sarcastic tone. "I also have every hope for her, but what good does that do? Any one may have great hopes for you, for me, for all of us, but at the same time he may be just as much wrong as right." . . . .

Twelve days later we reached Brest, and the day following Paris. The return passage was made without any misfortune, to the great displeasure of Dean Pitferge, who always expected to see the great ship wrecked.

And now, when I am sitting at my own table, if I had not my daily notes before me, I should think that the "Great Eastern," that floating city in which I lived for a month, the meeting of Ellen and Fabian, the peerless Niagara, all these were the visions of a dream. Ah! how delightful is travelling, "even when one does return," in spite of what the Doctor may say to the contrary.

For eight months I heard nothing of my original, but one day the post brought me a letter, covered with many-coloured stamps, which began with these words :—

"On board the 'Corinquay,' Auckland Rocks. At last we have been shipwrecked."

And ended thus :—

"Was never in better health.

"Very heartily yours,

"DEAN PITFERGE."

END OF "A FLOATING CITY."

THE BLOCKADE RUNNERS.

CHAPTER I.

THE " DOLPHIN."

THE Clyde was the first river whose waters were lashed into foam by a steam-boat. It was in 1812, when the steamer called the "Comet" ran between Glasgow and Greenock, at the speed of six miles an hour. Since that time more than a million of steamers or packet-boats have plied this Scotch river, and the inhabitants of Glasgow must be as familiar as any people with the wonders of steam navigation.

However, on the 3rd of December, 1862, an immense crowd, composed of ship-owners, merchants, manufacturers, workmen, sailors, women, and children, thronged the muddy streets of Glasgow, all going in the direction of

Kelvin Dock, the large ship-building premises belonging to Messrs. Tod and Mac Gregor. This last name especially proves that the descendants of the famous Highlanders have become manufacturers, and that they have made workmen of all the vassals of the old clan chieftains.

Kelvin Dock is situated a few minutes' walk from the town, on the right bank of the Clyde. Soon the immense timber-yards were thronged with spectators ; not a part of the quay, not a wall of the wharf, not a factory roof, showed an unoccupied place ; the river itself was covered with craft of all descriptions, and the heights of Govan, on the left bank, swarmed with spectators.

There was, however, nothing extraordinary in the event about to take place ; it was nothing but the launching of a ship, and this was an every-day affair with the people of Glasgow. Had the "Dolphin," then—for that was the name of the ship built by Messrs. Tod and Mac Gregor— some special peculiarity ? To tell the truth it had none.

It was a large ship, about 1500 tons, in which everything combined to obtain superior speed. Her engines, of 500-horse power, were from the workshops of Lancefield Forge ; they worked two screws, one on either side the stern-post, completely independent of each other. As for the depth of water the "Dolphin" would draw, it must be very inconsiderable ; connoisseurs were not deceived, and they concluded rightly that this ship was destined for

SHE PLUNGED INTO THE CLYDE.

shallow straits. But all these particulars could not in any way justify the eagerness of the people : taken altogether the " Dolphin " was nothing more or less than an ordinary ship. Would her launching present some mechanical diffi-culty to be overcome ? Not any more than usual. The Clyde had received many a ship of heavier tonnage, and the launching of the " Dolphin " would take place in the usual manner.

In fact, when the water was calm, the moment the ebb-tide set in, the workmen began to operate. Their mallets kept perfect time falling on the wedges meant to raise the ship's keel : soon a shudder ran through the whole of her massive structure ; although she had only been slightly raised, one could see that she shook, and then gradually began to glide down the well-greased wedges, and in a few moments she plunged into the Clyde. Her stern struck the muddy bed of the river, then she raised herself on the top of a gigantic wave, and, carried forward by her start, would have been dashed against the quay of the Govan timber-yards, if her anchors had not restrained her.

The launch had been perfectly successful, the " Dolphin" swayed quietly on the waters of the Clyde, all the spec-tators clapped their hands when she took possession of her natural element, and loud hurrahs arose from either bank.

But wherefore these cries and this applause? Undoubtedly the most eager of the spectators would have been at a loss to explain the reason of his enthusiasm. What was the cause, then, of the lively interest excited by this ship ? Simply the mystery which shrouded her destination ; it was not known to what kind of commerce she was to be appropriated, and in questioning different groups the diversity of opinion on this important subject was indeed astonishing.

However, the best informed, at least those who pretended to be so, agreed in saying that the steamer was going to take part in the terrible war which was then ravaging the United States of America, but more than this they did not know, and whether the " Dolphin " was a privateer, a transport ship, or an addition to the Federal marine, was what no one could tell.

" Hurrah ! " cried one, affirming that the " Dolphin " had been built for the Southern States.

" Hip ! hip ! hip ! " cried another, swearing that never had a faster boat crossed to the American coasts.

Thus its destination was unknown, and in order to obtain any reliable information one must be an intimate friend, or, at any rate, an acquaintance of Vincent Playfair and Co., of Glasgow.

A rich, powerful, intelligent house of business was that of Vincent Playfair and Co., in a social sense, an old and honourable family, descended from those tobacco lords who

built the finest quarters of the town. These clever mer
chants, by an act of the Union, had founded the first
Glasgow warehouse for dealing in tobacco from Virginia
and Maryland. Immense fortunes were realized; mills
and foundries sprang up in all parts, and in a few years
the prosperity of the city attained its height.

The house of Playfair remained faithful to the enterprising spirit of its ancestors, it entered into the most
daring schemes, and maintained the honour of English
commerce. The principal, Vincent Playfair, a man of fifty,
with a temperament essentially practical and decided,
although somewhat daring, was a genuine shipowner.
Nothing affected him beyond commercial questions, not
even the political side of the transactions, otherwise he
was a perfectly loyal and honest man.

However, he could not lay claim to the idea of building
and fitting up the " Dolphin ;" she belonged to his nephew,
James Playfair, a fine young man of thirty, the boldest
skipper of the British merchant marine.

It was one day at the Tontine coffee-room under the
arcades of the Town-hall, that James Playfair, after having
impatiently scanned the American journal, disclosed to
his uncle an adventurous scheme.

" Uncle Vincent," said he, coming to the point at once,
" there are two millions of pounds to be gained in less than
a month."

"And what to risk?" asked Uncle Vincent.

"A ship and a cargo."

"Nothing else?"

"Nothing, except the crew and the captain, and that does not reckon for much."

"Let us see," said Uncle Vincent.

"It is all seen," replied James Playfair. "You have read the *Tribune*, the *New York Herald*, the *Times*, the *Richmond Inquirer*, the *American Review*?"

"Scores of times, nephew."

"You believe, like me, that the war of the United States will last a long time still?"

"A very long time."

"You know how much this struggle will affect the interests of England, and especially those of Glasgow?"

"And more especially still the house of Playfair and Co.," replied Uncle Vincent.

"Theirs especially," added the young Captain.

"I worry myself about it every day, James, and I cannot think without terror of the commercial disasters which this war may produce; not but that the house of Playfair is firmly established, nephew; at the same time it has correspondents which may fail. Ah! those Americans, slaveholders or abolitionists, I have no faith in them!"

If Vincent Playfair was wrong in thus speaking with

respect to the great principles of humanity, always and everywhere superior to personal interests, he was, nevertheless, right in a commercial point of view. The most important material was failing at Glasgow, the cotton famine became every day more threatening, thousands of workmen were reduced to live upon public charity. Glasgow possessed 25,000 looms, by which 625,000 yards of cotton were spun daily ; that is to say, fifty millions of pounds yearly. From these numbers it may be guessed what disturbances were caused in the commercial part of the town, when the raw material failed altogether. Failures were hourly taking place, the manufactories were closed, and the workmen were dying of starvation.

It was the sight of this great misery which had put the idea of his bold enterprise into James Playfair's head.

"I will go for cotton, and will get it, cost what it may."

But as he also was a merchant as well as his uncle Vincent, he resolved to carry out his plan by way of exchange, and to make his proposition under the guise of a commercial enterprise.

"Uncle Vincent," said he, "this is my idea."

"Well, James ?"

"It is simply this ; we will have a ship built of superior sailing qualities and great bulk."

"That is quite possible."

"We will load her with ammunition of war, provisions, and clothes."

"Just so."

"I will take the command of this steamer, I will defy all the ships of the Federal marine for speed, and I will run the blockade of one of the southern ports."

"You must make a good bargain for your cargo with the Confederates, who will be in need of it," said his uncle.

"And I shall return laden with cotton."

"Which they will give you for nothing."

"As you say, uncle. Will it answer?"

"It will; but shall you be able to get there?"

"I shall, if I have a good ship."

"One can be made on purpose. But the crew?"

"Oh, I will find them. I do not want many men; enough to work with, that is all. It is not a question of fighting with the Federals, but distancing them."

"They shall be distanced," said uncle Vincent, in a peremptory tone; "but now, tell me, James, to what port of the American coast do you think of going?"

"Up to now, uncle, ships have run the blockade of New Orleans, Willmington, and Savannah, but I think of going straight to Charlestown; no English boat has yet been able to penetrate into the harbour, except the 'Bermuda.' I will do like her, and if my ship draws but very little water, I shall be able to go where the Federalists will not be able to follow."

"The fact is," said Uncle Vincent, "Charlestown is over-whelmed with cotton; they are even burning it to get rid of it."

"Yes," replied James; "besides, the town is almost invested, Beauregard is running short of provisions, and he will pay me a golden price for my cargo!"

"Well, nephew! and when will you start?"

"In six months; I must have the long winter nights to aid me."

"It shall be as you wish, nephew."

"It is settled, then, uncle?"

"Settled!"

"Shall it be kept quiet?"

"Yes; better so."

And this is how it was that five months later the steamer "Dolphin" was launched from the Kelvin Dock timber-yards, and no one knew her real destination.

CHAPTER II.

"GETTING UNDER SAIL."

THE "Dolphin" was rapidly equipped, her rigging was ready, and there was nothing to do but fit her up. She carried three schooner-masts, an almost useless luxury; in fact, the "Dolphin" did not rely on the wind to escape the Federalists, but rather on her powerful engines.

Towards the end of December a trial of the steamer was made in the gulf of the Clyde. Which was the most satisfied, builder or captain, it is impossible to say. The new steamer shot along wonderfully, and the patent log showed a speed of seventeen miles an hour, a speed which as yet no English, French, or American boat had ever obtained. The "Dolphin" would certainly have gained by several lengths in a sailing match with the fastest opponent.

The loading was begun on the 25th of December, the steamer having ranged along the steamboat-quay a little below Glasgow Bridge, the last which stretches across the Clyde before its mouth. Here the wharfs were heaped with a heavy cargo of clothes, ammunition, and provisions, which were rapidly carried to the hold of the " Dolphin." The nature of this cargo betrayed the mysterious destination of the ship, and the house of Playfair could no longer keep it secret ; besides, the "Dolphin" must not be long before she started. No American cruiser had been signalled in English waters ; and, then, when the question of getting the crew came, how was it possible to keep silent any longer ? They could not embark them even, without informing the men whither they were bound, for, after all, it was a matter of life and death, and when one risks one's life, at least it is satisfactory to know how and wherefore.

However, this prospect hindered no one ; the pay was good, and every one had a share in the speculation, so that a great number of the finest sailors soon presented themselves. James Playfair was only embarrassed which to choose, but he chose well, and in twenty-four hours his muster-roll bore the names of thirty sailors, who would have done honour to her Majesty's yacht.

The departure was settled for the 3rd of January ; on the 31st of December the " Dolphin " was ready, her hold full of ammunition and provisions, and nothing was keeping her now.

The skipper went on board on the 2nd of January, and was giving a last look round his ship with a Captain's eye, when a man presented himself at the fore part of the "Dolphin," and asked to speak with the Captain. One of the sailors led him on to the poop.

He was a strong, hearty-looking fellow, with broad shoulders and ruddy face, the simple expression of which ill concealed a depth of wit and mirth. He did not seem to be accustomed to a seafaring life, and looked about him with the air of a man little used to being on board a ship ; however, he assumed the manner of a Jack-tar, looking up at the rigging of the "Dolphin," and waddling in true sailor fashion.

When he had reached the Captain, he looked fixedly at him and said, " Captain James Playfair ? "

" The same," replied the skipper. " What do you want with me ? "

" To join your ship."

" There is no room ; the crew is already complete."

" Oh, one man, more or less, will not be in the way ; quite the contrary."

" You think so ? " said James Playfair, giving a sidelong glance at his questioner.

" I am sure of it," replied the sailor.

" But who are you ? " asked the Captain.

" A rough sailor, with two strong arms which, I can tell

"THE SAME," REPLIED THE SKIPPER.

you, are not to be despised on board a ship, and which I now have the honour of putting at your service."

"But there are other ships besides the 'Dolphin,' and other captains besides James Playfair. Why do you come here?"

"Because it is on board the 'Dolphin' that I wish to serve, and under the orders of Captain James Playfair."

"I do not want you."

"There is always need of a strong man, and if to prove my strength you will try me with three or four of the strongest fellows of your crew, I am ready."

"That will do," replied James Playfair. "And what is your name?"

"Crockston, at your service."

The Captain made a few steps backwards in order to get a better view of the giant, who presented himself in this odd fashion. The height, the build, and the look of the sailor did not deny his pretensions to strength.

"Where have you sailed?" asked Playfair of him.

"A little everywhere."

"And do you know where the 'Dolphin' is bound for?"

"Yes; and that is what tempts me."

"Ah, well! I have no mind to let a fellow of your stamp escape me. Go and find the first mate, and get him to enrol you."

P

Having said this the Captain expected to see the man turn on his heel and run to the bows, but he was mistaken. Crockston did not stir.

"Well! did you hear me?" asked the Captain.

"Yes, but it is not all," replied the sailor, "I have something else to ask you."

"Ah! You are wasting my time," replied James sharply; "I have not a moment to lose in talking."

"I shall not keep you long," replied Crockston, "two words more and that is all; I was going to tell you that I have a nephew."

"He has a fine uncle, then," interrupted James Playfair.

"Hah! Hah!" laughed Crockston.

"Have you finished?" asked the Captain, very impatiently.

"Well, this is what I have to say, when one takes the uncle, the nephew comes into the bargain."

"Ah! indeed!"

"Yes, that is the custom, the one does not go without the other."

"And what is this nephew of yours?"

"A lad of fifteen whom I am going to train to the sea; he is willing to learn, and will make a fine sailor some day."

"How now, Master Crockston," cried James Playfair; "do you think the 'Dolphin' is a training-school for cabin-boys?"

"Don't let us speak ill of cabin-boys: there was one of them who became Admiral Nelson, and another Admiral Franklin."

"Upon my honour, friend," replied James Playfair, "you have a way of speaking which I like; bring your nephew, but if I don't find the uncle the hearty fellow he pretends to be, he will have some business with me. Go, and be back in an hour."

Crockston did not want to be told twice; he bowed awkwardly to the Captain of the "Dolphin," and went on to the quay. An hour afterwards he came on board with his nephew, a boy of fourteen or fifteen, rather delicate and weakly-looking, with a timid and astonished air, which showed that he did not possess his uncle's self-possession and vigorous corporeal qualities. Crockston was even obliged to encourage him by such words as these:—

"Come," said he, "don't be frightened, they are not going to eat us, besides there is yet time to return."

"No, no," replied the young man, "and may God protect us!"

The same day the sailor Crockston and his nephew were inscribed in the muster-roll of the "Dolphin."

The next morning, at five o'clock, the fires of the steamer were well fed, the deck trembled under the vibrations of the boiler, and the steam rushed hissing through the escape-pipes. The hour of departure had arrived.

P 2

A considerable crowd in spite of the early hour flocked on the quays and on Glasgow Bridge, they had come to salute the bold steamer for the last time. Vincent Play-fair was there to say good-bye to Captain James, but he conducted himself on this occasion like a Roman of the good old times. His was a heroic countenance, and the two loud kisses with which he gratified his nephew were the indication of a strong mind.

"Go, James," said he to the young Captain, "go quickly, and come back quicker still; above all, don't abuse your position. Sell at a good price, make a good bargain, and you will have your uncle's esteem."

On this recommendation, borrowed from the manual of the perfect merchant, the uncle and nephew separated, and all the visitors left the boat.

At this moment Crockston and John Stiggs stood together on the forecastle, while the former remarked to his nephew, " This is well, this is well; before two o'clock we shall be at sea, and I have a good opinion of a voyage which begins like this."

For reply the novice pressed Crockston's hand.

James Playfair then gave the orders for departure.

" Have we pressure on ?" he asked of his mate.

"Yes, Captain," replied Mr. Mathew.

" Well, then, weigh anchor."

This was immediately done, and the screws began to

AND SOON DISAPPEARED.

Page 213.

move. The "Dolphin" trembled, passed between the ships in the port, and soon disappeared from the sight of the people, who shouted their last hurrahs.

The descent of the Clyde was easily accomplished, one might almost say that this river had been made by the hand of man, and even by the hand of a master. For sixty years, thanks to the dredges and constant dragging it has gained fifteen feet in depth, and its breadth has been tripled between the quays and the town. Soon the forests of masts and chimneys were lost in the smoke and fog ; the noise of the foundry hammers, and the hatchets of the timber-yards grew fainter in the distance. After the village of Patrick had been passed the factories gave way to country houses and villas. The "Dolphin," slackening her speed, sailed between the dykes which carry the river above the shores, and often through very narrow channel, which, however, is only a small inconvenience for a navigable river, for, after all, depth is of more importance than width. The steamer, guided by one of those excellent pilots from the Irish sea, passed without hesitation between floating buoys, stone columns, and *biggings*, surmounted with light-houses, which mark the entrance to the channel. Beyond the town of Renfrew, at the foot of Kilpatrick hills, the Clyde grew wider. Then came Bouling Bay, at the end of which opens the mouth of the canal which joins Edinburgh to Glasgow. Lastly, at the height of four hundred feet from the ground, was seen the outline of Dumbarton Castle, almost indiscernible through the mists, and soon the harbour-boats of Glasgow were rocked on the waves which the "Dolphin" caused. Some miles farther on Greenock, the birthplace of James Watt, was passed : the "Dolphin" now found herself at the mouth of the Clyde, and at the entrance of the gulf by which it empties its waters into the Northern Ocean. Here the first undulations of the sea were felt, and the steamer ranged along the picturesque coast of the Isle of Arran. At last the promontory of Cantyre, which runs out into the channel, was doubled ; the Isle of Rattelin was hailed, the pilot returned by a shore-boat to his cutter, which was cruising in the open sea ; the "Dolphin" returning to her Captain's authority, took a less frequented route round the north of Ireland, and soon, having lost sight of the last European land, found herself in the open ocean.

CHAPTER III.

THE " Dolphin " had a good crew, not fighting men, or boarding sailors, but good working men, and that was all she wanted. These brave, determined fellows were all, more or less, merchants ; they sought a fortune rather than glory ; they had no flag to display, no colours to defend with cannon ; in fact all the artillery on board consisted of two small swivel signal-guns.

The " Dolphin " shot bravely across the water, and fulfilled the utmost expectations of both builder and captain. Soon she passed the limit of British seas ; there was not a ship in sight ; the great Ocean route was free ; besides no ship of the Federal marine would have a right to attack her beneath the English flag. Followed she might be, and prevented from forcing the blockade, and precisely for this reason had James Playfair sacrificed everything to the speed of his ship, in order not to be pursued.

Howbeit a careful watch was kept on board, and in spite

of the extreme cold a man was always in the rigging ready
to signal the smallest sail that appeared on the horizon.
When evening came, Captain James gave the most precise
orders to Mr. Mathew.

" Don't leave the man on watch too long in the rigging,
the cold may seize him, and in that case it is impossible to
keep a good look-out ; change your men often."

" I understand, Captain," replied Mr. Mathew.

" Try Crockston for that work ; the fellow pretends
to have excellent sight; it must be put to trial ; put
him on the morning watch, he will have the morning
mists to see through.   If anything particular happens
call me."

This said, James Playfair went to his cabin.   Mr.
Mathew called Crockston, and told him the Captain's
orders.

" To-morrow, at six o'clock," said he, "you are to relieve
watch of the main-masthead."

For reply, Crockston gave a decided grunt, but Mr.
Mathew had hardly turned his back when the sailor muttered some incomprehensible words, and then cried,—

" What on earth did he say about the main-mast ?"

At this moment his nephew, John Stiggs, joined him on
the forecastle.

" Well, my good Crockston," said he.

" It's all right, all right," said the seaman, with a forced smile; "there is only one thing, this wretched boat shakes herself like a dog coming out of the water, and it makes my head confused."

" Dear Crockston, and it is for my sake."

" For you and him," replied Crockston, "but not a word about that, John; trust in God, and He will not forsake you."

So saying, John Stiggs and Crockston went to the sailor's berth, but the sailor did not lie down before he had seen the young novice comfortably settled in the narrow cabin which he had got for him.

The next day, at six o'clock in the morning, Crockston got up to go to his place; he went on deck, where the first officer ordered him to go up into the rigging, and keep good watch.

At these words the sailor seemed undecided what to do; then making up his mind, he went towards the bows of the "Dolphin."

"Well, where are you off to now?" cried Mr. Mathew.

" Where you sent me," answered Crockston.

" I told you to go to the main-mast."

"And I am going there," replied the sailor, in an unconcerned tone, continuing his way to the poop.

" Are you a fool?" cried Mr. Mathew, impatiently; " you are looking for the bars of the main on the foremast. You are like a cockney, who doesn't know how to twist a cat-o'-nine-tails, or make a splice. On board what ship can you have been, man? The main-mast, stupid, the main-mast!"

The sailors who had run up to hear what was going on, burst out laughing, when they saw Crockston's disconcerted look, as he went back to the forecastle.

" So," said he, looking up the mast, the top of which was quite invisible through the morning mists; "so, am I to climb up here?"

" Yes," replied Mr. Mathew, "and hurry yourself! By St. Patrick a Federal ship would have time to get her bowsprit fast in our rigging before that lazy fellow could get to his post. Will you go up?"

Without a word, Crockston got on the bulwarks with some difficulty; then he began to climb the rigging with most visible awkwardness, like a man who did not know how to make use of his hands or feet. When he had reached the top-gallant, instead of springing lightly on to it, he remained motionless, clinging to the ropes, as if he had been seized with giddiness. Mr. Mathew, irritated by his stupidity ordered him to come down immediately.

"That fellow there," said he to the boatswain, "has never been a sailor in his life. Johnston, just go and see what he has in his bundle."

The boatswain made haste to the sailor's berth.

In the meantime Crockston was with difficulty coming

down again, but his foot having slipped, he slid down the rope he had hold of, and fell heavily on the deck.

"Clumsy blockhead! land-lubber!" cried Mr. Mathew, by way of consolation. "What did you come to do on board the 'Dolphin'! Ah! you entered as an able seaman, and you cannot even distinguish the main from the foremast! I shall have a little talk with you."

Crockston made no attempt to speak; he bent his back like a man resigned for anything he might have to bear; just then the boatswain returned.

"This," said he to the first officer, "is all that I have found; a suspicious portfolio with letters."

"Give them here," said Mr. Mathew. "Letters with Federal stamps! Mr. Halliburtt, of Boston! An abolitionist! a Federalist! Wretch! you are nothing but a traitor, and have sneaked on board to betray us! Never mind, you will be paid for your trouble with the cat-o'-nine-tails! Boatswain, call the Captain, and you others, just keep an eye on that rogue there."

Crockston received these compliments with a hideous grimace, but he did not open his lips. They had fastened him to the capstan, and he could move neither hand nor foot.

A few minutes later James Playfair came out of his cabin and went to the forecastle, where Mr. Mathew immediately acquainted him with the details of the case.

"What have you to say?" asked James Playfair, scarcely able to restrain his anger.

"Nothing," replied Crockston.

"And what did you come on board my ship for?"

"Nothing."

"And what do you expect from me now?"

"Nothing."

"Who are you? An American, as these letters seem to prove?"

Crockston did not answer.

"Boatswain," said James Playfair, "fifty lashes with the cat-o'-nine-tails to loosen his tongue. Will that be enough, Crockston?"

"It will remain to be seen," replied John Stiggs' uncle without moving a muscle.

"Now then, come along, men," said the boatswain.

At this order, two strong sailors stripped Crockston of his woollen jersey; they had already seized the formidable weapon, and laid it across the prisoner's shoulders, when the novice, John Stiggs, pale and agitated, hurried on deck.

"Captain!" exclaimed he.

"Ah! the nephew!" remarked James Playfair.

"Captain," repeated the novice, with a violent effort to

"CAPTAIN!" EXCLAIMED HE.

Page 220.

steady his voice, " I will tell you what Crockston does not want to say. I will hide it no longer; yes, he is American, and so am I; we are both enemies of the slave-holders, but not traitors come on board to betray the 'Dolphin' into the hands of the Federalists."

"What did you come to do, then?" asked the Captain, in a severe tone, examining the novice attentively. The latter hesitated a few seconds before replying, then he said, "Captain, I should like to speak to you in private."

Whilst John Stiggs made this request, James Playfair did not cease to look carefully at him; the sweet young face of the novice, his peculiarly gentle voice, the delicacy and whiteness of his hands, hardly disguised by paint, the large eyes, the animation of which could not hide their tenderness—all this together gave rise to a certain suspicion in the Captain's mind. When John Stiggs had made his request, Playfair glanced fixedly at Crockston, who shrugged his shoulders; then he fastened a questioning look on the novice, which the latter could not withstand, and said simply to him, " Come."

John Stiggs followed the Captain on to the poop, and then James Playfair, opening the door of his cabin, said to the novice, whose cheeks were pale with emotion, " Be so kind as to walk in, miss."

John, thus addressed, blushed violently, and two tears rolled involuntarily down his cheeks.

"Don't be alarmed, miss," said James Playfair, in a gentle voice, " but be so good as to tell me how I come to have the honour of having you on board?"

The young girl hesitated a moment, then reassured by the Captain's look, she made up her mind to speak.

"Sir," said she, "I wanted to join my father at Charleston ; the town is besieged by land and blockaded by sea. I knew not how to get there, when I heard that the 'Dolphin' meant to force the blockade. I came on board your ship, and I beg you to forgive me if I acted without your consent, which you would have refused me."

" Certainly," said James Playfair.

" I did well, then, not to ask you," resumed the young girl, with a firmer voice.

The Captain crossed his arms, walked round his cabin, and then came back.

" What is your name ?" said he.

" Jenny Halliburtt."

" Your father, if I remember rightly the address on the letters, is he not from Boston?"

" Yes, sir."

" And a Northerner is thus in a southern town in the thickest of the war ?"

" My father is a prisoner; he was at Charleston when the first shot of the Civil War was fired, and the troops of the Union driven from Fort Sumter by the Confederates. My father's opinions exposed him to the hatred of the Slavist part, and by the order of General Beauregard he was imprisoned. I was then in England, living with a relation who has just died, and left alone with no help but that of Crockston, our faithful servant, I wished to go to my father and share his prison with him."

"What was Mr. Halliburtt, then?" asked James Playfair.

"A loyal and brave journalist," replied Jenny proudly, one of the noblest editors of the "Tribune," and the one who was the boldest in defending the cause of the negroes.

"An abolitionist," cried the Captain angrily; "one of those men, who, under the vain pretence of abolishing slavery, have deluged their country with blood and ruin."

"Sir!" replied Jenny Halliburtt, growing pale, "you are insulting my father; you must not forget that I stand alone to defend him."

The young Captain blushed scarlet; anger mingled with shame struggled in his breast; perhaps he would have answered the young girl, but he succeeded in restraining himself, and opening the door of the cabin, he called "Boatswain!"

The boatswain came to him directly.

"This cabin will henceforward belong to Miss Jenny Halliburtt; have a cot made ready for me at the end of the poop; that's all I want.

The boatswain looked with a stupefied stare at the young novice addressed in a feminine name, but on a sign from James Playfair he went out.

"And now, miss, you are at home," said the young Captain of the "Dolphin." Then he retired.

CHAPTER IV.

CROCKSTON'S TRICK.

IT was not long before the whole crew knew Miss Halli-hurtt's story, which Crockston was no longer hindered from telling. By the Captain's orders he was released from the capstan, and the cat-o'-nine-tails returned to its place.

"A pretty animal," said Crockston, "especially when it shows its velvety paws."

As soon as he was free, he went down to the sailors' berths, found a small portmanteau, and carried it to Miss Jenny; the young girl was now able to resume her feminine attire, but she remained in her cabin, and did not again appear on deck.

As for Crockston, it was well and duly agreed that, as he was no more a sailor than a horse-guard, he should be exempt from all duty on board.

In the meanwhile the "Dolphin," with her twin screws

cutting the waves, sped rapidly across the Atlantic, and there was nothing now to do but keep a strict look out. The day following the discovery of Miss Jenny's identity, James Playfair paced the deck at the poop with a rapid step ; he had made no attempt to see the young girl and resume the conversation of the day before.

Whilst he was walking to and fro, Crockston passed him several times, looking at him askant with a satisfied grin : he evidently wanted to speak to the Captain, and at last his persistent manner attracted the attention of the latter, who said to him, somewhat impatiently,—

" How now, what do you want ? You are turning round me like a swimmer round a buoy : when are you going to leave off ?"

" Excuse me, Captain," answered Crockston, winking, " I wanted to speak to you."

" Speak, then."

" Oh, it is nothing very much, I only wanted to tell you frankly that you are a good fellow at bottom."

" Why at bottom ?"

" At bottom and surface also."

" I don't want your compliments."

" I am not complimenting you, I shall wait to do that when you have gone to the end."

" To what end ?"

" To the end of your task."

" Ah! I have a task to fulfil?"

"Decidedly, you have taken the young girl and myself on board ; good. You have given up your cabin to Miss Halliburtt ; good. You released me from the cat-o'-nine-tails ; nothing could be better. You are going to take us straight to Charleston ; that's delightful, but it is not all."

"How not all?" cried James Playfair, amazed at Crockston's boldness.

"No, certainly not," replied the latter, with a knowing look, "the father is prisoner there."

" Well, what about that ?"

" Well, the father must be rescued."

" Rescue Miss Halliburtt's father ?"

"Most certainly, and it is worth risking something for such a noble man and courageous citizen as he."

"Master Crockston," said James Playfair, frowning, " I am not in the humour for your jokes, so have a care what you say."

"You misunderstand me, Captain," said the American. " I am not joking in the least, but speaking quite seriously. What I have proposed may at first seem very absurd to you ; when you have thought it over you will see that you cannot do otherwise."

" What, do you mean that I must deliver Mr. Halliburtt ?"

"Just so, you can demand his release of General Beauregard, who will not refuse you."

"But if he does refuse me?"

"In that case," replied Crockston, in a deliberate tone, "we must use stronger measures, and carry off the prisoner by force."

"So," cried James Playfair, who was beginning to get angry, "so, not content with passing through the Federal fleets and forcing the blockade of Charleston, I must run out to sea again from under the cannon of the forts, and this to deliver a gentleman I know nothing of, one of those Abolitionists whom I detest, one of those journalists who shed ink instead of their blood!"

"Oh! it is but a cannon-shot more or less!" added Crockston.

"Master Crockston," said James Playfair, "mind what I say; if ever you mention this affair again to me, I will send you to the hold for the rest of the passage, to teach you manners."

Thus saying the Captain dismissed the American, who went off murmuring, "Ah, well, I am not altogether displeased with this conversation: at any rate, the affair is broached; it will do, it will do!"

James Playfair had hardly meant it when he said an Abolitionist whom I detest; he did not in the least side with the Federals, but he did not wish to admit that the question of slavery was the predominant reason for the civil war of the United States, in spite of President

Lincoln's formal declaration. Did he then think that the Southern States, eight out of thirty-six, were right in separating when they had been voluntarily united? Not so; he detested the Northerners, and that was all; he detested them as brothers separated from the common family—true Englishmen—who had thought it right to do what he, James Playfair, disapproved of with regard to the United States: these were the political opinions of the Captain of the "Dolphin." But more than this, the American war interfered with him personally, and he had a grudge against those who had caused this war; one can understand, then, how he would receive a proposition to deliver an Abolitionist. thus bringing down on him the Confederates, with whom he pretended to do business.

However, Crockston's insinuation did not fail to disturb him, he cast the thought from him, but it returned unceasingly to his mind, and when Miss Jenny came on deck the next day for a few minutes, he dared not look her in the face.

And really it was a great pity, for this young girl with the fair hair and sweet, intelligent face deserved to be looked at by a young man of thirty. But James felt embarrassed in her presence; he felt that this charming creature who had been educated in the school of misfortune possessed a strong and generous soul; he understood that his silence towards her inferred a refusal to acquiesce in her dearest wishes; besides, Miss Jenny never looked out for James Playfair, neither did she avoid him. Thus for the first few days they spoke little or not at all to each other. Miss Halliburtt scarcely ever left her cabin, and it is certain she would never have addressed herself to the Captain of the "Dolphin" if it had not been for Crockston's strategy, which brought both parties together.

The worthy American was a faithful servant of the Halliburtt family, he had been brought up in his master's house and his devotion knew no bounds. His good sense equalled his courage and energy, and, as has been seen, he had a way of looking things straight in the face. He was very seldom discouraged, and could generally find a way out of the most intricate dangers with a wonderful skill.

This honest fellow had taken it into his head to deliver Mr. Halliburtt, to employ the Captain's ship, and the Captain himself for this purpose, and to return with him to England. Such was his intention, so long as the young girl had no other object than to rejoin her father and share his captivity. It was this Crockston tried to make the Captain understand, as we have seen, but the enemy had not yet surrendered, on the contrary.

"Now," said he, "it is absolutely necessary that Miss Jenny and the Captain come to an understanding; if they are going to be sulky like this all the passage we shall get nothing done: they must speak, discuss; let them dispute even, so long as they talk, and I'll be hanged if during their conversation James Playfair does not propose himself what he refused me to-day."

But when Crockston saw that the young girl and the young man avoided each other, he began to be perplexed.

"We must look sharp," said he to himself, and the morning of the fourth day he entered Miss Halliburtt's cabin, rubbing his hands with an air of perfect satisfaction.

"Good news!" cried he, "good news! You will never guess what the Captain has proposed to me. A very noble young man he is. Now try."

"Ah!" replied Jenny, whose heart beat violently, "has he proposed to—"

"To deliver Mr. Halliburtt, to carry him off from the Confederates, and bring him to England."

"Is it true?" cried Jenny.

"It is, as I say, miss. What a good-hearted man this James Playfair is! These English are either all good or all bad. Ah! he may reckon on my gratitude, and I am ready to cut myself in pieces if it would please him."

Jenny's joy was profound on hearing Crockston's words. Deliver her father! she had never dared to think of such a plan, and the Captain of the " Dolphin " was going to risk his ship and crew!

"That's what he is," added Crockston ; "and this, Miss Jenny, is well worth an acknowledgment from you."

" More than an acknowledgment," cried the young girl ; " a lasting friendship !"

And immediately she left the cabin to find James Playfair, and express to him the sentiments which flowed from her heart.

" Getting on by degrees," muttered the American.

James Playfair was pacing to and fro on the poop, and, as may be thought, he was very much surprised, not to say amazed, to see the young girl go up to him, her eyes moist with grateful tears, and holding out her hand to him saying,—

"Thank you, sir, thank you for your kindness, which I should never have dared to expect from a stranger."

" Miss," replied the Captain, as if he understood nothing of what she was talking, and could not understand, " I do not know—"

" Nevertheless, sir, you are going to brave many dangers, perhaps compromise your interests for me, and you have done so much already in offering me on board an hospitality to which I have no right whatever—"

" Pardon me, Miss Jenny," interrupted James Playfair, " but I protest again I do not understand your words ; I have acted towards you as any well-bred man would towards a lady, and my conduct deserves neither so many thanks nor so much gratitude."

"THANK YOU, SIR. THANK YOU."

"Mr. Playfair," said Jenny, "it is useless to pretend any longer; Crockston has told me all!"

"Ah!" said the Captain, "Crockston has told you all, then I understand less than ever the reason for your leaving your cabin, and saying these words which—"

Whilst speaking the Captain felt very much embarrassed; he remembered the rough way in which he had received the American's overtures, but Jenny, fortunately for him, did not give him time for further explanation; she interrupted him, holding out her hand and saying,—

"Mr. James, I had no other object in coming on board your ship except to go to Charleston, and there, however cruel the slave-holders may be, they will not refuse to let a poor girl share her father's prison, that was all; I had never thought of a return as possible; but since you are so generous as to wish for my father's deliverance, since you will attempt everything to save him, be assured you have my deepest gratitude."

James did not know what to do or what part to assume; he bit his lip; he dared not take the hand offered him; he saw perfectly that Crockston had compromised him, so that escape was impossible; at the same time he had no thoughts of delivering Mr. Halliburtt, and getting complicated in a disagreeable business: but how dash to the ground the hope which had arisen in this poor girl's heart? How refuse the hand which she held out to him with a feeling of such profound friendship? How change to tears of grief the tears of gratitude which filled her eyes?

So the young man tried to reply evasively, in a manner which would insure his liberty of action for the future.

"Miss Jenny," said he, "rest assured I will do everything in my power for—"

And he took the little hand in both of his, but with the gentle pressure he felt his heart melt and his head grow confused: words to express his thoughts failed him. He stammered out some incoherent words,—

"Miss—Miss Jenny—for you—"

Crockston, who was watching him, rubbed his hands, grinning and repeating to himself,—

"It will come! it will come! it has come!"

How James Playfair would have managed to extricate himself from his embarrassing position no one knows, but fortunately for him, if not for the "Dolphin," the man on watch was heard crying,—

"Ahoy, officer of the watch!"

"What now?" asked Mr. Mathew.

"A sail to windward!"

James Playfair, leaving the young girl, immediately sprang to the shrouds of the main-mast.

HE SAW DISTINCTLY.

Page 235.

CHAPTER V.

THE SHOT FROM THE "IROQUOIS," AND MISS JENNY'S ARGUMENTS.

UNTIL now the navigation of the "Dolphin" had been very fortunate. Not one ship had been signalled before the sail hailed by the man on watch.

The "Dolphin" was then in 32° 51' latitude, and 57° 43' west longitude. For forty-eight hours a fog which now began to rise had covered the ocean. If this mist favoured the "Dolphin" by hiding her course, it also prevented any observations at a distance being made, and, without being aware of it, she might be sailing side by side, so to speak, with the ships she wished most to avoid.

Now this is just what had happened, and when the ship was signalled she was only three miles to windward.

When James Playfair had reached the bars, he saw distinctly, through an opening in the mist, a large Federal corvette in full pursuit of the "Dolphin."

After having carefully examined her, the Captain came down on deck again, and called to the first officer.

"Mr. Mathew," said he, "what do you think of this ship?"

"I think, Captain, that it is a Federal cruiser, which suspects our intentions."

"There is no possible doubt of her nationality," said James Playfair. "Look!"

At this moment the starry flag of the North United States appeared on the gaff-yards of the corvette, and the latter asserted her colours with a cannon-shot.

"An invitation to show ours," said Mr. Mathew. "Well, let us show them; there is nothing to be ashamed of."

"What's the good?" replied James Playfair. "Our flag will hardly protect us, and it will not hinder those people from paying us a visit? No; let us go ahead."

"And go quickly," replied Mr. Mathew, "for if my eyes do not deceive me, I have already seen that corvette lying off Liverpool, where she went to watch the ships in building: my name is not Mathew, if that is not 'The Iroquois' on her taffrail."

"And is she fast?"

"One of the fastest vessels of the Federal marine."

"What guns does she carry?"

"Eight."

"Pooh."

"Oh, don't shrug your shoulders, Captain," said Mr.

Mathew, in a serious tone; "two out of those eight guns are rifled, one is a sixty-pounder on the forecastle, and the other a hundred-pounder on deck."

"Upon my soul!" exclaimed James Playfair, "they are Parrott's, and will carry three miles."

"Yes, and farther than that, Captain."

"Ah, well! Mr. Mathew, let their guns be sixty or only four-pounders, and let them carry three miles or five hundred yards, it is all the same if we can go fast enough to avoid their shot. We will show this 'Iroquois' how a ship can go when she is built on purpose to go. Have the fires well banked up, Mr. Mathew."

The first officer gave the Captain's orders to the engineer, and soon volumes of black smoke curled from the steamer's chimneys.

This proceeding did not seem to please the corvette, for she made the "Dolphin" the signal to lie to, but James Playfair paid no attention to this warning, and did not change his ship's course.

"Now," said he, "we shall see what the 'Iroquois' will do; there is a fine opportunity for her to try her guns, go ahead full speed!"

"Good!" exclaimed Mr. Mathew; "she will not be long in saluting us."

Returning to the poop, the Captain saw Miss Halliburtt sitting quietly near the bulwarks.

"Miss Jenny," said he, "we shall probably be chased by that corvette you see to windward, and as she will speak to us with shot, I beg to offer you my arm to take you to your cabin again."

"Thank you, very much, Mr. Playfair," replied the young girl, looking at him, "but I am not afraid of cannon-shots."

"However, miss, in spite of the distance, there may be some danger."

"Oh, I was not brought up to be fearful; they accustom us to everything in America, and I assure you that the shot from the 'Iroquois' will not make me lower my head."

"You are brave, Miss Jenny."

"Let us admit, then, that I am brave, and allow me to stay by you."

"I can refuse you nothing, Miss Halliburtt," replied the Captain, looking at the young girl's calm face.

These words were hardly uttered when they saw a line of white smoke issue from the bulwarks of the corvette; before the report had reached the "Dolphin" a projectile whizzed through the air in the direction of the steamer.

At about twenty fathoms from the "Dolphin" the shot, the speed of which had sensibly lessened, skimmed over the surface of the waves, marking its passage by a series of water-jets ; then, with another burst, it rebounded to a certain height, passed over the " Dolphin," grazing the mizen-yards on the starboard side, fell at thirty fathoms beyond, and was buried in the waves.

"By Jove!" exclaimed James Playfair, "we must get along ; another slap like that is not to be waited for."

"Oh!" exclaimed Mr. Mathew, "they will take some time to reload such pieces."

"Upon my honour, it is an interesting sight," said Crockston, who, with arms crossed, stood perfectly at his ease looking at the scene, "and to say they are friends who send such brandy-balls!"

"Ah! that's you," cried James Playfair, scanning the American from head to foot.

"It is me, Captain," replied the American, undisturbed. "I have come to see how these brave Federals fire ; not badly, in truth, not badly."

The Captain was going to answer Crockston sharply, but at this moment a second shot struck the sea on the starboard side.

"Good," cried James Playfair, "we have already gained two cables on this 'Iroquois.' Your friends sail like a buoy ; do you hear, Master Crockston ?"

"I will not say they don't," replied the American, "and for the first time in my life it does not fail to please me."

A third shot fell still farther astern, and in less than ten minutes the "Dolphin" was out of range of the corvette's guns.

"So much for patent-logs, Mr. Mathew," said James Playfair; "thanks to those shot we know how to rate our speed. Now have the fires lowered; it is not worth while to waste our coal uselessly."

"It is a good ship that you command," said Miss Halliburtt to the young Captain.

"Yes, Miss Jenny, my good 'Dolphin,' makes her seventeen knots, and before the day is over, we shall have lost sight of that corvette."

James Playfair did not exaggerate the sailing qualities of his ship, and the sun had not set before the masts of the American ship had disappeared below the horizon.

This incident allowed the Captain to see Miss Halliburtt's character in a new light; besides, the ice was broken, henceforward, during the whole of the voyage, the interviews between the Captain and his passenger were frequent and prolonged; he found her to be a young girl, calm, strong, thoughtful, and intelligent, speaking with great ease, having her own ideas about everything, and expressing her thoughts with a conviction which unconsciously penetrated James Playfair's heart.

She loved her country, she was zealous in the great cause of the Union, and expressed herself on the civil war in the United States with an enthusiasm of which no other woman would have been capable. Thus it happened, more than once, that James Playfair found it difficult to answer her, even when questions purely mercantile arose in connexion with the war : Miss Jenny attacked them none the less vigorously, and would come to no other terms whatever. At first James argued a great deal, and tried to uphold the Confederates against the Federals, to prove that the Secessionists were in the right, and that if the people were united voluntarily they might separate in the same manner. But the young girl would not yield on this point; she demonstrated that the question of slavery was predominant in the struggle between the North and South Americans, that it was far more a war in the cause of morals and humanity than politics, and James could make no answer. Besides, during these discussions, which he listened to attentively, it is difficult to say whether he was more touched by Miss Halliburtt's arguments, or the charming manner in which she spoke ; but at last he was obliged to acknowledge, among other things, that slavery was the principal feature in the war, that it must be put an end to decisively, and the last horrors of barbarous times abolished.

It has been said that the political opinions of the Captain did not trouble him much. He would have sacrificed his most serious opinion before such enticing arguments

R

and under like circumstances; he made a good bargain of his ideas for the same reason, but at last he was attacked in his tenderest point : this was the question of the traffic in which the "Dolphin" was being employed, and, consequently, the ammunition which was being carried to the Confederates.

" Yes, Mr. James," said Miss Halliburtt, "gratitude does not hinder me from speaking with perfect frankness ; on the contrary, you are a brave seaman, a clever merchant, the house of Playfair is noted for its respectability ; but in this case it fails in its principles, and follows a trade unworthy of it."

" How ! " cried James, " the house of Playfair ought not to attempt such a commercial enterprise ? "

" No! it is taking ammunition to the unhappy creatures in revolt against the government of their country, and it is lending arms to a bad cause."

" Upon my honour, Miss Jenny, I will not discuss the right of the Confederates with you ; I will only answer you with one word : I am a merchant, and as such I only occupy myself with the interests of my house; I look for gain wherever there is an opportunity of getting it."

"That is precisely what is to be blamed, Mr. James," replied the young girl; "profit does not excuse it; thus, when you supply arms to the Southerners, with which to continue a criminal war, you are quite as guilty as when you sell opium to the Chinese, which stupefies them."

" Oh! for once, Miss Jenny, this is too much, and I cannot admit—"

" No ; what I say is just, and when you consider it, when you understand the part you are playing, when you think of the results for which you are responsible, you will yield to me in this point, as in so many others."

James Playfair was dumbfoundered at these words ; he left the young girl, a prey to angry thoughts, for he felt his powerlessness to answer ; then he sulked like a child for half an hour, and an hour later he returned to the singular young girl who could overwhelm him with convincing arguments, with quite a pleasant smile.

In short, however it may have come about, and although he would not acknowledge it to himself, Captain James Playfair belonged to himself no longer, he was no longer commander-in-chief on board his own ship.

Thus, to Crockston's great joy, Mr. Halliburtt's affairs appeared to be in a good way ; the Captain seemed to have decided to undertake everything in his power to deliver Miss Jenny's father, and for this he would be obliged to compromise the " Dolphin," his cargo, his crew, and incur the displeasure of his worthy uncle Vincent.

CHAPTER VI.

SULLIVAN ISLAND CHANNEL.

Two days after the meeting with the "Iroquois," the "Dolphin" found herself abreast of the Bermudas, where she was assailed by a violent squall. These isles are frequently visited by hurricanes, and are celebrated for shipwrecks. It is here that Shakspeare has placed the exciting scene of his drama, "The Tempest," in which Ariel and Caliban dispute for the empire of the floods.

The squall was frightful; James Playfair thought once of running for one of the Bermudas, where the English had a military post: it would have been a sad waste of time, and therefore especially to be regretted; happily the "Dolphin" behaved herself wonderfully well in the storm, and after flying a whole day before the tempest, she was able to resume her course towards the American coast.

But if James Playfair had been pleased with his ship, he

THE SQUALL.

Page 144.

had not been less delighted with the young girl's bravery ;
Miss Halliburtt had passed the worst hours of the storm
at his side, and James knew that a profound, imperious,
irresistible love had taken possession of his whole being.

"Yes," said he, "this brave girl is mistress on board ;
she turns me like the sea a ship in distress—I feel that I am
foundering! What will Uncle Vincent say ? Ah! poor
nature, I am sure that if Jenny asked me to throw all this
cursed cargo into the sea, I should do it without hesitating,
for love of her."

Happily for the firm of Playfair and Co., Miss Halliburtt
did not demand this sacrifice ; nevertheless, the poor Captain
had been taken captive, and Crockston, who read his
heart like an open book, rubbed his hands gleefully.

"We will hold him fast!" he muttered to himself, "and
before a week has passed my master will be quietly
installed in one of the best cabins of the 'Dolphin.'"

As for Miss Jenny, did she perceive the feelings which she
inspired ? did she allow herself to share them ? No one
could say, and James Playfair least of all ; the young girl
kept a perfect reserve, and her secret remained deeply
buried in her heart.

But whilst love was making such progress in the heart
of the young Captain, the "Dolphin" sped with no less
rapidity towards Charleston.

On the 13th of January, the watch signalled land ten

miles to the west. It was a low-lying coast, and almost blended with the line of the sea in the distance. Crockston was examining the horizon attentively, and about nine o'clock in the morning he cried,—

" Charleston light-house ! "

Now that the bearings of the "Dolphin" were set, James Playfair had but one thing to do, to decide by which channel he would run into Charleston Bay.

" If we meet with no obstacles," said he, " before three o'clock we shall be in safety in the docks of the port."

The town of Charleston is situated on the banks of an estuary seven miles long and two broad, called Charleston Harbour, the entrance to which is rather difficult. It is enclosed between Morris Island on the south, and Sullivan Island on the north. At the time when the "Dolphin" attempted to force the blockade Morris Island already belonged to the Federal troops, and General Gillmore had caused batteries to be erected overlooking the harbour. Sullivan Island, on the contrary, was in the hands of the Confederates, who were also in possession of Moultrie Fort, situated at the extremity of the island ; therefore it would be advantageous to the " Dolphin " to go as close as possible to the northern shores to avoid the firing from the forts on Morris Island.

Five channels led into the estuary, Sullivan Island Channel, the Northern Channel, the Overall Channel, the

CROCKSTON WAS EXAMINING THE HORIZON ATTENTIVELY.

Pa. 14'

Principal Channel, and lastly, the Lawford Channel ; but it was useless for strangers, unless they had skilful pilots on board, or ships drawing less than seven feet of water to attempt this last ; as for Northern and Overall Channels, they were in range of the Federalist batteries, so that it was no good thinking of them. If James Playfair could have had his choice, he would have taken his steamer through the Principal Channel, which was the best, and the bearings of which were easy to follow ; but it was necessary to yield to circumstances, and to decide according to the event. Besides, the Captain of the " Dolphin " knew perfectly all the secrets of this bay, its dangers, the depths of its water at low tide, and its currents, so that he was able to steer his ship with the greatest safety as soon as he entered one of these narrow straits. The great question was to get there.

Now this work demanded an experienced seaman, and one who knew exactly the qualities of the " Dolphin."

In fact two Federal frigates were now cruising in the Charleston waters. Mr. Mathew soon drew James Playfair's attention to them.

" They are preparing to ask us what we want on these shores," said he.

" Ah, well ! we won't answer them," replied the Captain, " and they will not get their curiosity satisfied."

In the meanwhile the cruisers were coming on full steam

towards the "Dolphin," who continued her course, taking
care to keep out of range of their guns. But in order
to gain time James Playfair made for the south-west,
wishing to put the enemies' ships off their guard ; the latter
must have thought that the "Dolphin" intended to make
for Morris Island Channel. Now there they had batteries
and guns, a single shot from which would have been
enough to sink the English ship ; so the Federals allowed
the "Dolphin" to run towards the south-west, contenting
themselves by observing her without following closely.

Thus for an hour the respective situations of the ships did
not change, for James Playfair, wishing to deceive the
cruisers as to the course of the "Dolphin," had caused the
fires to be moderated, so that the speed was decreased.
However, from the thick volumes of smoke which escaped
from the chimneys, it might have been thought that he was
trying to get his maximum pressure, and, consequently, his
maximum of rapidity.

"They will be slightly astonished presently," said
James Playfair, "when they see us slip through their
fingers!"

In fact, when the Captain saw that he was near enough to
Morris Island, and before a line of guns, the range of which
he did not know, he turned his rudder quickly, and the ship
resumed her northerly course, leaving the cruisers two
miles to windward of her ; the latter seeing this manœuvre

understood the steamer's object, and began to pursue her in earnest, but it was too late. The " Dolphin " doubled her speed under the action of the screws, and distanced them rapidly. Going nearer to the coast, a few shell were sent after her as an acquittal of conscience, but the Federals were outdone, for their projectiles did not reach half way. At eleven o'clock in the morning, the steamer ranging near Sullivan Island, thanks to her small draft, entered the narrow strait full steam ; there she was in safety, for no Federalist cruiser dared follow her in this channel, the depth of which, on an average, was only eleven feet at low tide.

" How ?" cried Crockston, "and is that the only difficulty ?"

" Oh ! oh ! Master Crockston," said James Playfair, "the difficulty is not in entering, but in getting out again."

" Nonsense !" replied the American, " that does not make me at all uneasy ; with a boat like the ' Dolphin ' and a Captain like Mr. James Playfair, one can go where one likes, and come out in the same manner."

Nevertheless, James Playfair, with telescope in his hand, was attentively examining the route to be followed. He had before him excellent coasting guides, with which he could go a-head without any difficulty or hesitation.

Once his ship safely in the narrow channel which runs the length of Sullivan Island, James steered bearing towards the middle of Fort Moultrie as far as the Pickney Castle, situated on the isolated island of Shute's Folly; on the other side rose Fort Johnson, a little way to the north of Fort Sumter.

At this moment the steamer was saluted by some shot which did not reach her, from the batteries on Morris Island. She continued her course without any deviation, passed before Moultrieville, situated at the extremity of Sullivan Island, and entered the bay.

Soon Fort Sumter on the left protected her from the batteries of the Federalists.

This fort, so celebrated in the civil war, is situated three miles and a half from Charleston, and about a mile from each side of the bay: it is nearly pentagonal in form, built on an artificial island of Massachusetts granite, it took ten years to construct and cost more than 900,000 dollars.

It was from this fort, on the 13th of April, 1861, that Anderson and the Federal troops were driven, and it was against it that the first shot of the Confederates was fired. It is impossible to estimate the quantity of iron and lead which the Federals showered down upon it. However, it resisted for almost three years, but a few months after the passage of the "Dolphin," it fell beneath General Gillmore's three hundred-pounders on Morris Island.

MISS HALLIBURTT WAS STANDING ON THE POOP.

Page 251.

But at this time it was in all its strength, and the Confederate flag floated proudly above it.

Once past the fort the town of Charleston appeared lying between Ashley and Cooper rivers.

James Playfair threaded his way through the buoys which mark the entrance of the channel, leaving behind the Charleston lighthouse visible above Morris Island. He had hoisted the English flag, and made his way with wonderful rapidity through the narrow channels. When he had passed the Quarantine buoy, he advanced freely into the centre of the bay. Miss Halliburtt was standing on the poop, looking at the town where her father was kept prisoner, and her eyes filled with tears.

At last the steamer's speed was moderated by the Captain's orders; the "Dolphin" ranged along the end of the south and east batteries, and was soon moored at the quay of the North Commercial Wharf.

CHAPTER VII.

A SOUTHERN GENERAL.

THE "Dolphin" on arriving at the Charleston quay, had
been saluted by the cheers of a large crowd. The inhabitants of this town, strictly blockaded by sea, were not
accustomed to visits from European ships. They asked
each other, not without astonishment, what this great
steamer, proudly bearing the English flag, had come to do
in their waters ; but when they learned the object of her
voyage, and why she had just forced the passage Sullivan,
when the report spread that she carried a cargo of smuggled
ammunition, the cheers and joyful cries were redoubled.

James Playfair, without losing a moment, entered into
negotiation with General Beauregard, the military commander of the town. The latter eagerly received the young
Captain of the "Dolphin," who had arrived in time to
provide the soldiers with the clothes and ammunition they
were so much in want of. It was agreed that the unload-

ing of the ship should take place immediately, and numerous hands came to help the English sailors.

Before quitting his ship James Playfair had received from
Miss Halliburtt the most pressing injunctions with regard
to her father, and the Captain had placed himself entirely
at the young girl's service.

"Miss Jenny," he had said, "you may rely on me; I
will do the utmost in my power to save your father, but I
hope this business will not present many difficulties ; I shall
go and see General Beauregard to-day, and without asking
him at once for Mr. Halliburtt's liberty, I shall learn in
what situation he is, whether he is on bail, or a prisoner."

"My poor father!" replied Jenny, sighing; "he little
thinks his daughter is so near him. Oh that I could fly into
his arms!"

"A little patience, Miss Jenny, you will soon embrace
your father. Rely upon my acting with the most entire
devotion, but also with prudence and consideration."

This is why James Playfair, after having delivered
the cargo of the "Dolphin" up to the General, and
bargained for an immense stock of cotton, faithful to
his promise, turned the conversation to the events of
the day.

"So," said he, "you believe in the triumph of the slave-
holders ?"

"I do not for a moment doubt of our final success, and as

regards Charleston, Lee's army will soon relieve it; besides, what do you expect from the Abolitionists? admitting that which will never be, that the commercial towns of Virginia, the two Carolinas, Georgia, Alabama, fall under their power, what then? Will they be masters of a country they can never occupy? No, certainly not; and for my part if they are ever victorious they shall pay dearly for it."

"And you are quite sure of your soldiers?" asked the Captain; "you are not afraid that Charleston will grow weary of a siege which is ruining her?"

"No, I do not fear treason; besides, the traitors would be punished remorselessly, and I would destroy the town itself by sword or fire if I discovered the least Unionist movement. Jefferson Davis confided Charleston to me, and you may be sure that Charleston is in safe hands."

"Have you any Federal prisoners?" asked James Playfair, coming to the interesting object of the conversation.

"Yes, Captain," replied the General, "it was at Charleston that the first shot of separation was fired. The Abolitionists who were here attempted to resist, and after being defeated they have been kept as prisoners of war."

"And have you many?"

"About a hundred."

"Free in the town?"

"They were until I discovered a plot formed by them:

their chief succeeded in establishing a communication with the besiegers, who were thus informed of the situation of affairs in the town. I was then obliged to lock up these dangerous guests, and several of them will only leave their prison to ascend the slope of the citadel, where ten confederate balls will reward them for their federalism "

"What ! to be shot !" cried the young man, shuddering involuntarily.

" Yes, and their chief first of all. He is a very dangerous man to have in a besieged town. I have sent his letters to the President at Richmond, and before a week is passed hi; sentence will be irrevocably passed."

"Who is this man you speak of," asked James Playfair, with an assumed carelessness.

"A journalist from Boston, a violent Abolitionist with the confounded spirit of Lincoln."

"And his name ?"

"Jonathan Halliburtt."

"Poor wretch !" exclaimed James, suppressing his emotion; "whatever he may have done one cannot help pitying him. And you think that he will be shot ?"

"I am sure of it," replied Beauregard. "What can you expect ? War is war, one must defend oneself as best one can."

"Well, it is nothing to me," said the Captain ; "I shall be far enough away when this execution takes place."

"What! you are thinking of going away already."

"Yes, General, business must be attended to; as soon as my cargo of cotton is on board I shall be out to sea again. I was fortunate enough to enter the bay, but the difficulty is in getting out again. The 'Dolphin' is a good ship; she can beat any of the Federal ships for speed, but she does not pretend to distance cannon-balls, and a shell in her hull or engine would seriously affect my enterprise."

"As you please, Captain," replied Beauregard; "I have no advice to give you under such circumstances. You are doing your business, and you are right. I should act in the same manner were I in your place; besides a stay at Charleston is not very pleasant, and a harbour where shells are falling three days out of four is not a safe shelter for your ship; so you will set sail when you please; but can you tell me what is the number and the force of the Federal ships cruising before Charleston?"

James Playfair did his best to answer the General, and took leave of him on the best of terms; then he returned to the "Dolphin" very thoughtful and very depressed from what he had just heard.

"What shall I say to Miss Jenny? ought I to tell her of Mr. Halliburtt's terrible situation? or would it be better to keep her in ignorance of the trial which is awaiting her? Poor child!"

He had not gone fifty steps from the governor's house

when he ran against Crockston : the worthy American had
been watching for him since his departure.

"Well, Captain?"

James Playfair looked steadily at Crockston, and the
latter soon understood he had no favourable news to give
him.

"Have you seen Beauregard?" he asked.

"Yes," replied James Playfair.

"And have you spoken to him about Mr. Halliburtt?"

"No! it was he who spoke to me about him."

"Well, Captain?"

"Well! I may as well tell you everything, Crockston."

"Everything, Captain."

"General Beauregard has told me that your master will
be shot within a week."

At this news any one else but Crockston would have
grown furious or given way to bursts of grief, but the
American, who feared nothing, only said, with almost a
smile on his lips,—

"Pooh! what does it matter?"

"How! what does it matter?" cried James Playfair; "I
tell you that Mr. Halliburtt will be shot within a week, and
you answer. what does it matter?"

"And I mean it—if in six days he is on board the
'Dolphin,' and if in seven days the 'Dolphin' is on the open
sea."

S

"Right!" exclaimed the Captain, pressing Crockston's hand. "I understand, my good fellow, you have got some pluck; and for myself, in spite of Uncle Vincent, I would throw myself overboard for Miss Jenny."

"No one need be thrown overboard," replied the American, "only the fish would gain by that: the most important business now is to deliver Mr. Halliburtt."

"But you must know that it will be difficult to do so."

"Pooh!" exclaimed Crockston.

"It is a question of communicating with a prisoner strictly guarded."

"Certainly."

"And to bring about an almost miraculous escape."

"Nonsense," exclaimed Crockston; "a prisoner thinks more of escaping than his guardian thinks of keeping him; that's why, thanks to our help, Mr. Halliburtt will be saved."

"You are right, Crockston."

"Always right."

"But now what will you do? there must be some plan: and there are precautions to be taken."

"I will think about it."

"But when Miss Jenny learns that her father is condemned to death, and that the order for his execution may come any day—"

"She will know nothing about it, that is all."

"Yes, it will be better for her and for us to tell her nothing."

"Where is Mr. Halliburtt imprisoned?" asked Crockston.

"In the citadel," replied James Playfair.

"Just so!—On board now?"

"On board, Crockston!"

CHAPTER VIII.

THE ESCAPE.

MISS JENNY, sitting at the poop of the "Dolphin." was anxiously waiting the captain's return; when the latter went up to her she could not utter a word, but her eyes questioned James Playfair more eagerly than her lips could have done. The latter, with Crockston's help, informed the young girl of the facts relating to her father's imprisonment. He said that he had carefully broached the subject of the prisoners of war to Beauregard, but as the General did not seem disposed at all in their favour, he had thought it better to say no more about it, but think the matter over again.

"Since Mr. Halliburtt is not free in the town, his escape will be more difficult.; but I will finish my task, and I promise you, Miss Jenny, that the 'Dolphin' shall not leave Charleston, without having your father on board."

"I PROMISE YOU, MISS JENNY."

"Thank you, Mr. James; I thank you with my whole heart."

At these words James Playfair felt a thrill of joy through his whole being.

He approached the young girl with moist eyes and quivering lips; perhaps he was going to make an avowal of the sentiments he could no longer repress, when Crockston interfered,—

"This is no time for grieving," said he; "we must go to work, and consider what to do."

"Have you any plan, Crockston?" asked the young girl.

"I always have a plan," replied the American: "it is my peculiarity."

"But a good one?" said James Playfair.

"Excellent! and all the ministers in Washington could not devise a better; it is almost as good as if Mr. Halliburtt was already on board."

Crockston spoke with such perfect assurance, at the same time with such simplicity, that it must have been the most incredulous person who could doubt his words.

"We are listening, Crockston," said James Playfair.

"Good! You, Captain, will go to General Beauregard, and ask a favour of him which he will not refuse you."

"And what is that?"

"You will tell him that you have on board a tiresome

subject, a scamp who has been very troublesome during the voyage, and excited the crew to revolt. You will ask of him permission to shut him up in the citadel; at the same time on the condition that he shall return to the ship on her departure, in order to be taken back to England, to be delivered over to the justice of his country."

" Good !" said James Playfair, half smiling, "I will do all that, and Beauregard will grant my request very willingly."

" I am perfectly sure of it," replied the American.

" But," resumed Playfair, " one thing is wanting."

" What is that ? "

" The scamp."

" He is before you, Captain."

" What, the rebellious subject ?—"

" Is myself; don't trouble yourself about that."

" Oh ! you brave, generous heart," cried Jenny, pressing the American's rough hands between her small white palms.

" Go, Crockston," said James Playfair; " I understand you, my friend ; and I only regret one thing, that is, that I cannot take your place."

" Every one his part," replied Crockston; "if you put yourself in my place you would be very much embarrassed, which I shall not be; you will have enough to do later on to get out of the harbour under the fire of the Feds

and Rebs, which, for my part, I should manage very
badly."

" Well, Crockston, go on."

" Once in the citadel—I know it—I shall see what to do,
and rest assured I shall do my best ; in the meanwhile, you
will be getting your cargo on board."

" Oh ! business is now a very unimportant detail," said
the Captain.

" Not at all ! and what would your uncle Vincent say to
that ?   We must join sentiment with work ; it will prevent suspicion ; but do it quickly. Can you be ready in
six days ? "

" Yes."

" Well, let the 'Dolphin' be ready to start on the
22nd."

" She shall be ready."

" On the evening of the 22nd of January, you understand, send a shore-boat with your best men to White
Point, at the end of the town ; wait there till nine o'clock,
and then you will see Mr. Halliburtt and your servant."

" But how will you manage to effect Mr. Halliburtt's
deliverance, and also escape yourself ? "

" That's my look-out."

" Dear Crockston, you are going to risk your life then,
to save my father ! "

"Don't be uneasy, Miss Jenny, I shall risk absolutely nothing, you may believe me."

"Well," asked James Playfair, "when must I have you locked up?"

"To-day—you understand—I demoralize your crew; there is no time to be lost."

" Would you like any money? it may be of use to you in the citadel."

"Money to buy the gaoler! Oh, no! it would be a poor bargain; when one goes there the gaoler keeps the money and the prisoner! No! I have surer means than that; however, a few dollars may be useful; one must be able to drink, if needs be."

"And intoxicate the gaoler."

"No, an intoxicated gaoler would spoil everything. No, I tell you I have an idea, let me work it out."

"Here, my good fellow, are ten dollars."

"It is too much, but I will return what is over."

"Well, then, are you ready?"

"Quite ready to be a downright rogue."

"Let us go to work then."

"Crockston," said the young girl, in a faltering voice, "you are the best man on earth."

I know it," replied the American, laughing good-humouredly. "By-the-bye, Captain, an important item."

" What is that ? "

" If the General proposes to hang your rebel—you know that military men like sharp work—"

" Well, Crockston ?"

" Well, you will say that you must think about it."

" I promise you I will."

The same day to the great astonishment of the crew, who were not in the secret, Crockston with his feet and hands in irons was taken on shore by a dozen sailors, and half-an-hour after, by Captain James Playfair's request, he was led through the streets of the town, and in spite of his resistance was imprisoned in the citadel.

During this and the following days the unloading of the "Dolphin" was rapidly accomplished ; the steam cranes lifted out the European cargo to make room for the native goods. The people of Charleston, who were present at this interesting work, helped the sailors, whom they held in great respect, but the Captain did not leave the brave fellows much time for receiving compliments ; he was constantly behind them, and urged them on with a feverish activity, the reason of which the sailors could not suspect.

Three days later, on the 18th of January, the first bales of cotton began to be packed in the hold : although James Playfair troubled himself no more about it, the firm of Playfair and Co. were making an excellent bargain having obtained the cotton which encumbered the Charleston wharves at very far less than its value.

In the meantime no news had been heard of Crockston. Jenny without saying anything about it was a prey to incessant fears, her pale face spoke for her, and James Playfair endeavoured his utmost to ease her mind.

" I have all confidence in Crockston," said he, " he is a devoted servant, as you must know better than I do, Miss Jenny. You must make yourself quite at ease ; believe me, in three days you will be folded in your father's arms."

"Ah ! Mr. James," cried the young girl, "how can I ever repay you for such devotion ? How shall we ever be able to thank you ? "

"I will tell you when we are in English seas," replied the young Captain.

Jenny raised her tearful face to him for a moment, then her eyelids drooped, and she went back to her cabin.

James Playfair hoped that the young girl would know nothing of her father's terrible situation until he was in safety, but she was apprized of the truth by the involuntary indiscretion of a sailor.

The reply from the Richmond cabinet had arrived by a courier who had been able to pass the line of outposts the reply contained Jonathan Halliburtt's death-warrant. The news of the approaching execution was not long in spreading through the town, and it was brought on board by one of the sailors of the "Dolphin;" the man told the Captain, without thinking that Miss Halliburtt was within hearing ; the young girl uttered a piercing cry, and fell unconscious on the deck. James Playfair carried her to her cabin, but the most assiduous care was necessary to restore her to life.

When she opened her eyes again, she saw the young Captain, who, with a finger on his lips, enjoined absolute silence. With difficulty she repressed the outburst of her grief, and James Playfair, leaning towards her, said gently,—

"Jenny, in two hours your father will be in safety near you, or I shall have perished in endeavouring to save him!"

Then he left the cabin, saying to himself, "And now he must be carried off at any price, since I must pay for his liberty with my own life and that of my crew."

The hour for action had arrived, the loading of the cotton cargo had been finished since morning ; in two hours the ship would be ready to start.

James Playfair had left the North Commercial Wharf and gone into the roadstead, so that he was ready to make use of the tide, which would be high at nine o'clock in the evening.

It was seven o'clock when James left the young girl

and began to make preparations for departure. Until the present time the secret had been strictly kept between himself, Crockston, and Jenny; but now he thought it wise to inform Mr. Mathew of the situation of affairs, and he did so immediately.

"Very well, sir," replied Mr. Mathew, without making the least remark, "and nine o'clock is the time ? "

" Nine o'clock, and have the fires lit immediately, and the steam got up."

"It shall be done, Captain."

"The 'Dolphin' may remain at anchor; we will cut our moorings and sheer off. without losing a moment."

"Just so."

" Have a lantern placed at the mainmast-head; the night is dark, and will be foggy; we must not risk losing our way in returning; you had better have the bell for starting rung at nine o'clock."

"Your orders shall be punctually attended to, Captain."

"And now, Mr. Mathew, have a shore-boat manned with six of our best men; I am going to set out directly for 'White Point.' I leave Miss Jenny in your charge, and may God protect us! "

"May God protect us!" repeated the first officer.

Then he immediately gave the necessary orders for the fires to be lighted, and the shore-boat provided with men.

In a few minutes the boat was ready, and James Playfair, after bidding Jenny good-bye, stepped into it, whilst
at the same time, he saw volumes of black smoke issuing
from the chimneys of the ship, and losing itself in the fog.

The darkness was profound ; the wind had fallen, and
in the perfect silence the waters seemed to slumber in
the immense harbour, whilst a few uncertain lights glimmered through the mist. James Playfair had taken his
place at the rudder, and with a steady hand he guided
his boat towards White Point. It was a distance of about
two miles ; during the day James had taken his bearings
perfectly, so that he was able to make direct for Charleston Point.

Eight o'clock struck from the church of St. Philip when
the shore-boat ran aground at White Point.

There was an hour to wait before the exact time fixed
by Crockston ; the quay was deserted, with the exception
of the sentinel pacing to and fro on the south and east
batteries. James Playfair grew impatient, and the minutes
seemed hours to him.

At half-past eight he heard the sound of approaching
steps ; he left his men with their oars clear and ready
to start, and went himself to see who it was ; but he had
not gone ten feet when he met a band of coast-guards,
in all about twenty men. James drew his revolver from
his waist, deciding to make use of it, if needs be ; but

what could he do against these soldiers, who were coming on to the quay?

The leader came up to him, and seeing the boat, asked,—

"Whose craft is that?"

"It is a shore-boat belonging to the 'Dolphin,' replied the young man.

"And who are you?"

"Captain James Playfair."

"I thought you had already started, and were now in the Charleston channels."

"I am ready to start. I ought even now to be on my way, but—"

"But—" persisted the coast-guard.

A bright idea shot through James's mind, and he answered,—

"One of my sailors is locked up in the citadel, and to tell the truth I had almost forgotten him; fortunately I thought of him in time, and I have sent my men to bring him."

"Ah! that troublesome fellow; you wish to take him back to England?"

"Yes."

"He might as well be hung here as there," said the coast-guard, laughing at his joke.

"So I think," said James Playfair, "but it is better to have the thing done in the regular way."

MR. HALLIBURTT?

Page 271.

"Not much chance of that, Captain, when you nave to face the Morris Island batteries."

"Don't alarm yourself. I got in and I'll get out again."

"Prosperous voyage to you!"

"Thank you."

With this the men went off, and the shore was left silent.

At this moment nine o'clock struck; it was the appointed moment. James felt his heart beat violently: a whistle was heard; he replied to it, then ne waited, listening, with his hand up to enjoin perfect silence on the sailors; a man appeared enveloped in a large cloak, and looking from one side to another, James ran up to him.

"Mr. Halliburtt?"

"I am he," replied the man with the cloak.

"God be praised!" cried James Playfair; "embark without losing a minute. Where is Crockston?"

"Crockston!" exclaimed Mr. Halliburtt, amazed. "What do you mean?"

"The man who has saved you and brought you here was your servant Crockston."

"The man who came with me was the gaoler from the citadel," replied Mr. Halliburt.

"The gaoler!" cried James Playfair.

Evidently he knew nothing about it, and a thousand fears crowded in his mind.

"Quite right, the gaoler," cried a well-known voice; "the gaoler is sleeping like a top in my cell."

"Crockston! you! can it be you?" exclaimed Mr. Halliburtt.

"No time to talk now, master; we will explain everything to you afterwards; it is a question of life or death. Get in quick!"

The three men took their places in the boat.

"Push off!" cried the captain.

Immediately the six oars dipped into the water; the boat darted like a fish through the waters of Charleston Harbour.

CHAPTER IV.

"BETWEEN TWO FIRES."

THE boat. pulled by six robust oarsmen. flew over the water. The fog was growing dense, and it was with difficulty that James Playfair succeeded in keeping to the line of his bearings. Crockston sat at the bows, and Mr. Halliburtt at the stern next the Captain. The prisoner, only now informed of the presence of his servant, wished to speak to him, but the latter enjoined silence.

However, a few minutes later. when they were in th middle of the harbour, Crockston determined to speak knowing what thoughts were uppermost in Mr. Halliburtt' mind.

"Yes, my dear master," said he, "the gaoler is in my place in the cell, where I gave him two smart blows, one on the head and the other on the stomach, to act as a sleeping draught, and this when he was bringing me my supper; there is gratitude for you. I took his clothes and his keys,

T

found you, and let you out of the citadel, under the soldiers'
noses. That is all I have done."

"But my daughter?—" asked Mr. Halliburtt.

"Is on board the ship which is going to take you to
England."

"My daughter there! there!" cried the American,
springing from his seat.

"Silence!" replied Crockston, "a few minutes, and we
shall be saved."

The boat flew through the darkness, but James Playfair was obliged to steer rather by guess, as the lanterns
of the "Dolphin" were no longer visible through the fog.
He was undecided what direction to follow, and the darkness was so great that the rowers could not even see to the
end of their oars.

"Well, Mr. James?" said Crockston.

"We must have made more than a mile and a half,"
replied the Captain. "You don't see anything, Crockston?"

"Nothing; nevertheless I have good eyes, but we shall
get there all right. They don't suspect anything out
there."

These words were hardly finished when the flash of a gun
gleamed for an instant through the darkness, and vanished
in the mist.

"A signal!" cried James Playfair.

JENNY FELL INTO HER FATHER'S ARMS.

Page 275.

"Whew!" exclaimed Crockston, "it must have come from the citadel. Let us wait."

A second, then a third shot was fired in the direction of the first, and almost the same signal was repeated a mile in front of the shore-boat.

"That is from Fort Sumter," cried Crockston, "and it is the signal of escape. Urge on the men; everything is discovered."

"Pull for your lives, my men!" cried James Playfair, urging on the sailors, "those gun-shots cleared my route. 'The Dolphin' is eight hundred yards ahead of us. Stop! I hear the bell on board. Hurrah, there it is again! Twenty pounds for you if we are back in five minutes!"

The boat skimmed over the waves under the sailors' powerful oars. A cannon boomed in the direction of the town. Crockston heard a ball whiz past them.

The bell on the "Dolphin" was ringing loudly. A few more strokes and the boat was alongside. A few more seconds and Jenny fell into her father's arms.

The shore-boat was immediately raised, and James Playfair sprang on to the poop.

"Is the steam up, Mr. Mathew?"

"Yes, Captain."

"Have the moorings cut at once."

A few minutes later the two screws carried the steamer towards the principal channel, away from Fort Sumter.

"Mr. Mathew," said James, "we must not think of taking the Sullivan Island channel; we should run directly under the Confederate guns. Let us go as near as possible to the right side of the harbour out of range of the Federal batteries. Have you a safe man at the helm?"

"Yes, Captain."

"Have the lanterns and the fires on deck extinguished; there is a great deal too much light, but we cannot help the reflection from the engine-rooms."

During this conversation "the Dolphin" was going at a great speed; but in altering her course to keep to the right side of the Charleston Harbour she was obliged to enter a channel which took her for a moment near Fort Sumter; and when scarcely half a mile off all the guns bearing on her were discharged at the same time, and a shower of shot and shell passed in front of the "Dolphin" with a thundering report.

"Too soon, stupids," cried James Playfair, with a burst of laughter. "Make haste, make haste, Mr. Engineer! We shall get between two fires."

The stokers fed the furnaces, and the "Dolphin" trembled all over with the effort of the engine as if she was on the point of exploding.

At this moment a second report was heard, and another shower of balls whizzed behind the "Dolphin."

"Too late, stupids," cried the young Captain, with a regular roar.

Then Crockston, who was standing on the poop, cried, "That's one passed. A few minutes more, and we shall have done with the Rebs."

"Then do you think we have nothing more to fear from Fort Sumter ?" asked James.

"Nothing at all, but everything from Fort Moultrie, at the end of Sullivan Island ; but they will only get a chance at us for half a minute, and then they must choose their time well, and shoot straight if they want to reach us. We are getting near."

"Right ; the position of Fort Moultrie will allow us to go straight for the principal channel. Fire away then, fire away !"

At the same moment, and as if in obedience to James Playfair, the fort was illuminated by a triple line of lightning. A frightful crash was heard ; then a crackling sound on board the steamer.

"Touched this time !" exclaimed Crockston.

"Mr. Mathew !" cried the Captain to his second, who was stationed at the bows, "what has been damaged ?"

"The bowsprit broken."

"Any wounded ?"

"No, Captain."

"Well, then, the masts may go to Jericho. Straight

into the pass ! Straight ! and steer towards the island."

"We have passed the Rebs !" cried Crockston; "and if we must have balls in our hull, I would much rather have the Northerners ; they are more easily digested."

In fact, the "Dolphin" could not yet consider herself out of danger; for if Morris Island was not fortified with the formidable pieces of artillery which were placed there a few months later, nevertheless its guns and mortars could easily have sunk a ship like the "Dolphin."

The alarm had been given to the Federals on the island, and to the blockading squadron, by the firing from Forts Sumter and Moultrie. The besiegers could not make out the reason of this night attack ; it did not seem to be directed against them. However, they were obliged to consider it so, and were ready to reply.

It occupied James Playfair's thoughts whilst making towards the passes of Morris Island ; and he had reason to fear, for in a quarter of an hour's time lights gleamed rapidly through the darkness. A shower of small shell fell round the steamer, scattering the water over her bulwarks ; some of them even struck the deck of the "Dolphin," but not on their points, which saved the ship from certain ruin. In fact, these shell, as it was afterwards discovered, could break into a hundred fragments, and each cover a superficial area of a hundred and twenty square feet with Greek fire, which would burn for twenty minutes, and nothing could extinguish it. One of these shell alone could set a ship on fire. Fortunately for the "Dolphin," they were a new invention, and as yet far from perfect. Once thrown into the air, a false rotary movement kept them inclined, and, when falling, instead of striking on their points, where is the percussion apparatus, they fell flat. This defect in construction alone saved the "Dolphin." The falling of these shells did her little harm, and under the pressure of her over-heated boilers she continued to advance into the pass.

At this moment, and in spite of his orders, Mr. Halliburtt and his daughter went to James Playfair on the poop; the latter urged them to return to their cabins, but Jenny declared that she would remain by the Captain. As for Mr. Halliburtt, who had just learnt all the noble conduct of his deliverer, he pressed his hand without being able to utter a word.

The "Dolphin" was speeding rapidly towards the open sea. There were only three miles more before she would be in the waters of the Atlantic; if the pass was free at its entrance, she was saved. James Playfair was wonderfully well acquainted with all the secrets of Charleston Bay, and he guided his ship through the darkness with an unerring hand. He was beginning to think his daring enterprise successful, when a sailor on the forecastle cried,—

"A ship!"

"A ship?" cried James.

"Yes, on the larboard side."

The fog had cleared off, and a large frigate was seen making towards the pass, in order to obstruct the passage of the "Dolphin." It was necessary, cost what it might, to distance her, and urge the steam-engine to an increase of speed, or all was lost.

"Port the helm at once!" cried the Captain.

Then he sprang on to the bridge above the engine. By his orders one of the screws was stopped, and under the action of the other the "Dolphin," veering with an extraordinary rapidity avoided running foul of the frigate, and advanced like her to the entrance of the pass. It was now a question of speed.

James Playfair understood that in this lay his own safety, Miss Jenny's, her father's, and that of all his crew.

The frigate was considerably in advance of the "Dolphin." It was evident from the volumes of black smoke issuing from her chimneys that she was getting up her steam. James Playfair was not the man to be left in the background.

"How are the engines?" cried he to the engineer.

"At the maximum speed," replied the latter; "the steam is escaping by all the valves."

"Fasten them down," ordered the Captain.

And his orders were executed at the risk of blowing up the ship.

The " Dolphin " again increased her speed ; the pistons worked with frightful rapidity; the metal plates on which the engine was placed trembled under the terrific force of their blows. It was a sight to make the boldest shudder.

"More pressure!" cried James Playfair ; "put on more pressure !"

" Impossible !" replied the engineer ; " the valves are tightly closed ; our furnaces are full up to the mouths."

"What difference! Fill them with cotton soaked in spirits ; we must pass that frigate at any price."

At these words the most daring of the sailors looked at each other, but did not hesitate. Some bales of cotton were thrown into the engine-room, a barrel of spirits broached over them, and this expensive fuel placed, not without danger, in the red-hot furnaces. The stokers could no longer hear each other speak for the roaring of the flames. Soon the metal plates of the furnaces became red-hot ; the pistons worked like the pistons of a locomotive ; the steam-gauge showed a frightful tension ; the steamer flew over the water ; her boards creaked, and her chimneys threw out volumes of smoke mingled with flames. She was going at a headlong speed, but, nevertheless, she was gaining on the frigate—passed her, distanced her, and in ten minutes was out of the channel.

" Saved ! " cried the Captain.

" Saved ! " echoed the crew, clapping their hands.

Already the Charleston beacon was disappearing in the south-west ; the sound of firing from the batteries grew fainter, and it might with reason be thought that the danger was all past, when a shell from a gun-boat cruising at large was hurled whizzing through the air. It was easy to trace its course, thanks to the line of fire which followed it.

Then was a moment of anxiety impossible to describe , every one was silent, and each watched fearfully the arch described by the projectile. Nothing could be done to escape it, and in a few seconds it fell with a frightful noise on the fore-deck of the " Dolphin."

The terrified sailors crowded to the stern, and no one dared move a step, whilst the shell was burning with a brisk crackle.

But one brave man alone among them ran up to the formidable weapon of destruction. It was Crockston ; he took the shell in his strong arms, whilst showers of sparks were falling from it ; then, with a superhuman effort, he threw it overboard.

HE TOOK THE SHELL.

Page 281

Hardly had the shell reached the surface of the water when it burst with a frightful report.

" Hurrah! hurrah!" cried the whole crew of the " Dolphin " unanimously, whilst Crockston rubbed his hands.

Some time later the steamer sped rapidly through the waters of the Atlantic; the American coast disappeared in the darkness, and the distant lights which shot across the horizon indicated that the attack was general between the batteries of Morris Island and the forts of Charleston Harbour

CHAPTER X.

ST. MUNGO.

THE next day at sunrise the American coast had disap-peared; not a ship was visible on the horizon, and the " Dolphin," moderating the frightful rapidity of her speed, made quietly towards the Bermudas.

It is useless to recount the passage across the Atlantic, which was marked by no accidents, and ten days after the departure from Queenstown the French coast was hailed.

What passed between the Captain and the young girl may be imagined, even by the least observant individuals. How could Mr. Halliburtt acknowledge the devotion and courage of his deliverer, if it was not by making him the happiest of men ? James Playfair did not wait for English seas to declare to the father and daughter the sentiments which overflowed his heart, and, if Crockston is to be believed, Miss Jenny received his confession with a happi-ness she did not try to conceal.

Thus it happened that on the 14th of February, 18—, a numerous crowd was collected in the dim aisles of St. Mungo, the old cathedral of Glasgow.   There were seamen, merchants, manufacturers, magistrates, and some of every denomination, gathered here.   There was Miss Jenny in bridal array, and beside her the worthy Crockston, resplendent in apple-green clothes, with gold buttons, whilst Uncle Vincent stood proudly by his nephew.

In short, they were celebrating the marriage of James Playfair, of the firm of Vincent Playfair and Co., of Glasgow, with Miss Jenny Halliburtt, of Boston.

The ceremony was accomplished amidst great pomp. Every one knew the history of the " Dolphin," and every one thought the young Captain well recompensed for his devotion.   He alone said that his reward was greater than he deserved.

In the evening there was a grand ball and banquet at Uncle Vincent's house, with a large distribution of shillings to the crowd collected in Gordon Street.   Crockston did ample justice to this memorable feast, while keeping himself perfectly within bounds.

Every one was happy at this wedding ; some at their own happiness, and others at the happiness around them, which is not always the case at ceremonies of this kind.

Late in the evening, when the guests had retired, James Playfair took his uncle's hand.

"Well, Uncle Vincent," said he to him.

"Well, Nephew James?"

"Are you pleased with the charming cargo I brought you on board the 'Dolphin'?" continued Captain Playfair, showing him his brave young wife.

"I am quite satisfied," replied the worthy merchant; "I have sold my cotton at three hundred and seventy-five per cent. profit."

THE END.

"WELL, UNCLE VINCENT."

1758737R0022

Printed in Great Britain
by Amazon.co.uk, Ltd.,
Marston Gate.